VENGEANCE

VENGEANCE

A NOVEL BY

KATE BRIAN

New York   London   Toronto   Sydney

SIMON & SCHUSTER BFYR

An imprint of Simon & Schuster Children's Publishing Division
1230 Avenue of the Americas, New York, New York 10020

For information about special discounts for bulk purchases, please
contact Simon & Schuster Special Sales at 1-866-506-1949 or
business@simonandschuster.com.
The Simon & Schuster Speakers Bureau can bring authors to your live
event. For more information or to book an event, contact the Simon &
Schuster Speakers Bureau at 1-866-248-3049 or visit
our website at www.simonspeakers.com.

alloyentertainment
Produced by Alloy Entertainment
151 West 26th Street, New York, NY 10001

Typography by Liz Dresner
The text of this book was set in Filosofia.
Manufactured in the United States of America
2 4 6 8 10 9 7 5 3 1
Library of Congress Control Number: 2011930749
ISBN 978-1-4169-8473-3
ISBN 978-1-4424-1289-7 (eBook)

FIRST EDITION

To all the fans who have shown me and Reed such love and support over the past few years and sixteen books, this one's for you

VENGEANCE

IMAGINING THE POSITIVE

The sky that early June day was the kind of blue that goes on forever and makes you believe anything is possible. As I stood at the edge of the new Billings House construction site—my boyfriend, Josh Hollis, holding my hand, and my sister and best friend, Noelle Lange, standing just to my right—I felt like that particular blue had been conjured just for me.

It was all happening. Billings was being rebuilt. A huge, yellow backhoe was clearing the plot, bringing up the dark, wet earth of spring with each drag of its shovel, releasing the sweet scent of new beginnings into the air. Construction workers in hard hats marked off the area, unloaded cement blocks and workbenches, and walked in and out of trailers, letting the doors slam purposefully behind them. It was the fresh start I had always hoped for, and I couldn't stop smiling. I reached up and touched the gold locket hanging around my neck— the one that had once belonged to my ancestor, Eliza Williams—with this warm, comforting sense that I was exactly where I was supposed to be, doing exactly what I was supposed to be doing.

"Reed, are you *sure* this is a good idea?" Josh asked, squeezing my hand.

My smile faltered. He squinted his green eyes against the sun as he turned to look at me. His light blue sweater had a few drops of yellow paint on the collar and his always unruly, dark blond hair was pushed up in the back by the breeze. Josh was, hands down, the hottest guy at Easton Academy—the most handsome, adorable, mature, attentive guy I'd ever met—even when he was raining on my parade.

"It just seems so . . . wrong," Noelle added.

I gaped at her. Her dark hair was back in a low ponytail and she wore a black boatneck dress over black boots. Not very bright-and-bold, spring-fashion runway, but Noelle had never been one for color in her wardrobe. And, of course, she looked perfect anyway.

"Unbelievable. *This* is what you guys finally agree on?" I gestured toward the construction site. The two of them rolled their eyes at each other.

"It's just . . . when Daddy left you all that money, I don't think this is what he had in mind."

Noelle looked down at the ground, nudging a pebble of old-Billings concrete with the pointed toe of her boot. This had been a habit of hers for the past couple of months, ever since her father—*our* father—had been murdered the night of my seventeenth birthday. She looked down whenever she spoke of him. Actually, she looked down a lot more often than she ever had before. I knew how much she missed him. I missed him too, but in a different way. Noelle had spent every day of her nineteen years knowing him, loving him, calling him "Dad."

I, however, had never really gotten to know him. I missed what I had never had the chance to have. Sometimes I wasn't sure which was worse, until I saw the way Noelle's face fell whenever he came up in conversation. At those moments I knew her loss was far greater than mine. At least the crazy bitch who'd done it, Alyssa Kane—the mother of our now-deceased Billings sister Cheyenne Martin—had been given a speedy trial and sentenced to life in prison after a mere ten-minute deliberation by the jury. Guess that's what happens when you stab someone right in front of two dozen witnesses, including about ten cops.

Of course, the dagger had been meant for me, a fact that I tried not to think about.

My phone rang for about the millionth time that day. Another demanding alumna, no doubt. I had invited every living Billings alum and some of the more influential Easton graduates to the ribbon-cutting ceremony this weekend and had planned a cocktail reception and brunch as well, hoping to show them all such a good time that they'd go back into the world and spread nothing but good PR for Billings. But the simple weekend I'd hoped for was turning into a circus. All the wealthy, influential women from Billings's past had special requirements or demands that they absolutely *had* to have fulfilled before their arrival in Connecticut, and each time my phone rang or beeped or vibrated, my nerves frayed a little thinner.

Noelle gave my bag the stink eye, so I reached inside the outer pocket and hit ignore. Whoever it was, I could return the call when I got back to my dorm.

"This is our chance, Noelle," I said gently. "Thanks to your dad, we can remake Billings into what we always knew it could be."

"I know. You've said all this before," Noelle remarked impatiently as the backhoe beeped loudly, backing toward the far edge of the plot. "But my father—I mean, *our* father . . . he hated this place. Don't you think it's a tad crass to be using his money to rebuild it?"

My mouth suddenly tasted sour. How could she not remember that this whole thing had been her idea? Back before my birthday, back when Mr. Lange was still alive, she was the one who had suggested I ask him for the money to rebuild Billings as my birthday gift. She had known then how much he hated Billings, and she'd still tried to pressure me to do it anyway. But now that the Easton Board of Directors had granted me the building rights—after accepting my offer of a huge cash donation to the school, of course—it was like she'd forgotten all about her initial involvement.

But I couldn't remind her of it, because I knew it was all coming from a place of sadness and regret. I knew that she was just trying to honor her dad's wishes now that he was gone. I got that. I did. I just wished it could be different. I wished I could find a way to win her over. Because rebuilding Billings without her support just felt . . . wrong.

"Well, I think that he would understand," I said, turning to gaze out across the upturned earth. I saw my construction chief, Larry

Genovese, shake hands with another burly man. "I think he would appreciate that I want to do things right this time. I want Billings to be a place we can all be proud of. There's going to be an actual application process now. I'm going to make sure that girls are admitted based on their merits, like GPA, school involvement, community service—"

Noelle scoffed, but I wasn't sure if she was laughing at my Girl Scout version of the new Billings, or if she was annoyed that I was dissing the old ways.

"And I'll be making the final decisions even after I graduate," I said, looking at Josh. "It won't be a bunch of girls talking behind each other's backs, accepting people based on catty, shallow criteria like who was the first to snag the latest limited edition Gucci bag."

"Oh, so now you're qualified to decide what it takes to be a Billings Girl?" Noelle said snarkily.

My face burned. I was about to reply when my phone rang again. Frustrated, I tugged it from my bag. The caller ID read "Janice Winthrop." One of Billings's wealthiest alums. She was supposed to be coming in for the ribbon-cutting ceremony and had RSVP'd yes to both the cocktail hour at Mitchell Hall Saturday night and the brunch in town on Sunday morning. Now my heart all but stopped, hoping she wasn't calling to cancel. I was counting on both her financial and moral support once Billings was up and running. This was one call I could not ignore.

"Hang on a sec, you guys." I brought the phone to my ear. "Hello, this is Reed," I said in my most professional voice.

"Reed, hi! Janice Winthrop here. I'm so sorry to bother you again, but I just called the Driscoll to confirm my reservation, and they have me in a business suite rather than the royal suite, and they swear someone else has booked it. I'd have my assistant look into it, but he comes down with these migraines at just *the* worst moments."

I somehow felt both relieved and even tenser, all at the same time. At least she was still coming. The logistics I could deal with. "I'll call them right away, Ms. Winthrop," I promised. "I'll have it all worked out before you arrive."

"Good. Thank you, Reed. I'm so looking forward to meeting you in person and seeing all my old friends!" Ms. Winthrop said. "Our reunions always take place on the week of my firm's board meetings, so I can never make them. I can't thank you enough for getting everyone together like this!"

I pressed my lips together. Interesting how she made it sound as if this whole thing were being put on for her benefit. But all I said was, "It's my pleasure. I'm looking forward to meeting you, too."

"All right, then. See you on Saturday!"

There was a click and the line went dead. I looked down at the phone and noticed that I also had twenty-five new texts and thirty new e-mails, all from Billings alums, no doubt. I felt my skin growing warm and my shoulder muscles coiling, and I told myself to relax. I could answer all their questions and concerns later. Right now, Janice Winthrop was the pressing issue.

I was about to speed-dial the Driscoll Hotel, when a puffy cloud moved in front of the sun, and an awful chill went down my back.

Someone was watching at me. I could feel it. Standing still as stone, I scanned the campus, and something moved in the corner of my eye. I turned quickly, just in time to see a shock of blond hair as it disappeared around the corner of the library. My hands went clammy. My heart was in my throat.

"Who was that?" Noelle asked from behind.

For a split second I thought she'd seen the blond girl too—the girl who looked so much like Ariana Osgood, I could hardly catch my breath. But then I realized she was referring to my call.

From this distance it could have been anyone, I told myself. *Don't start looking for ways to freak yourself out now.*

"Janice Winthrop. Just confirming her plans," I replied lightly, tossing my phone back in my bag. For some reason, I didn't want Noelle to see me sweat, and the Driscoll call could wait a few minutes. I turned around and tried to remember what we had been talking about before the interruption.

"Ah, Janice Winthrop. One of the most notoriously needy Billings Girls of all time," Noelle commented, crossing her slim arms over her chest. "Don't let her get too involved, or your phone will never stop ringing."

I narrowed my eyes at her as the sun emerged again. Right. We'd been talking about how unqualified I was to choose the new residents of Billings.

"Noelle, I've told you a million times that you could help me make all the decisions about Billings. I'd make you a full partner like that," I said, snapping my fingers.

Noelle took a deep breath and blew it out audibly. She tilted her head up and stared at the sky, letting her ponytail tumble down her back, taking in all that blue. For a second I thought that the gorgeousness of the day was working its magic on her and she was finally going to agree, that she was going to give me her blessing and offer to help—an offer I could sorely use now that things were really getting under way. Mr. Lange's business partner, Chester Worth, had helped me a ton—finding the architect and hiring the contractors and the project's accountant—but there were decisions to be made every day, and as much as I put on a competent front, sometimes I felt like I was in way over my head.

"I don't think so," she said finally, leveling her chin again. She shook her head. "In the end, this place brought us more misery than anything else. You were almost murdered at Billings, Reed, in case you've forgotten. It's where Sabine tortured you, where she killed Cheyenne. . . ." She drew a pair of dark Donna Karan sunglasses out of her bag and slipped them on. Only then did she turn to fully face me, when I couldn't see her eyes at all. "Honestly? I'm glad Hathaway had it torn down."

My mouth went completely dry. She couldn't be serious. Billings was her life for two and a half years. Yes, some awful things had happened there, but Billings had also brought us together, made us friends, and in a way made us sisters. But before my stunned brain could formulate a response, she'd turned on her spiked heels and was striding across campus. Josh put his arms around me from behind and gave me a squeeze.

"I can't believe she just said that," I told him. My chest was all hollow, like she'd punched a hole right through it.

"Hey. Noelle wouldn't be Noelle if she wasn't a stubborn bitch," he joked, nuzzling my ear.

I tilted my head away from him and turned around. "You get why I'm doing this, right?" I said, looking up into his eyes. "I mean, I know you hated what Billings was, but it's not going to be like that anymore. Not with me in charge."

"I know." He leaned in to kiss my lips. "Forget what I said before. I'm proud of you. You're taking something negative and imagining the positive possibilities. Not a lot of people would bother."

I grinned. "Wow. Thanks."

"Anytime."

He kissed me again, this time longer and deeper and so perfectly that I almost forgot where I was until one of the construction workers whistled at us, eliciting a round of applause from his coworkers. Josh blushed and I lifted a hand.

"Yeah, yeah. Get back to work!" I shouted jokingly.

Josh checked his phone. "Actually, I should be getting back to work too. I have a lot of studying to do this week."

"You do realize you already got into Cornell," I said, taking his hand as we started toward the center of campus. "Plus you're, like, a shoo-in to win half the senior awards at the banquet next week. Give yourself a break already."

Josh's face reddened all over again. "Yeah, about the awards ceremony . . . I'm not even sure I'm going to make it."

I blinked. The end-of-the-year Easton Academy awards ceremony was the biggest school-sanctioned event of the year. All the
seniors' parents came, plus a bunch of alumni, and everyone got
dressed to the nines to watch one another receive awards for academic achievement, leadership, philanthropy, and athletics. Aside
from graduation, it was the most anticipated event of the final
semester, and Josh was one of the senior class's shining stars. He
should've been psyched.

"You can't not go," I said, placing my hands on his chest. "Who's
going to collect all your hard-earned bling?"

Josh smirked, but looked away. "I have my bio final at eight the
next morning and I want to ace it. I'm sorry, but I don't want to be one
of those losers who slack off just because they can."

"Okay," I said, knitting my brow. I'd never heard of a second-
semester senior working as hard as he was. We paused at the intersec-
tion of two stone pathways, one leading to the library and administration
buildings, the other back toward the dorms. "Well, then . . . I guess I'll
see you at dinner later?"

"Definitely," he said with what seemed like a relieved smile.

I was just letting go of his hand when my phone rang. I fished it out
of the outer pocket of my leather messenger bag and blinked. It was
one of the Easton Academy numbers, but not one I recognized. Josh
gave me a quizzical look as I answered.

"Hello?"

"Miss Brennan? This is Headmaster Hathaway."

My heart skipped a startled beat.

"Oh. Hi, Headmaster," I said, looking at Josh.

"Double H?" Josh mouthed, confused. I shrugged.

"I need to see you in my office," the Headmaster said, his tone making my toes curl and my fingers clench. *"Now."*

SHELVED

"If you have to study, you can go," I told Josh as we hurried up the marble steps inside Hell Hall, which was the not-so-affectionate nickname the students of Easton had for Hull Hall, where all the teachers kept their offices. Behind closed doors, phones rang, keyboards clacked, and muffled conversations were carried on. "I'm sure it's nothing."

"Didn't sound like nothing," Josh said, jogging behind me. "I can spare a few minutes."

I looked over my shoulder at him with a grateful smile. "Thanks."

Just then, someone came around the corner on the stairwell and slammed into my shoulder, hard. Missy Thurber, former Billings Girl and class-A bitch, was coming down the stairs and didn't even bother to mutter an apology.

"Ow! Don't worry! I'll just get out of your way!" I called after her sarcastically.

She paused on the landing below and shot me a serious and silent look of death. One that actually sent a chill through my heart. Then she kept right on walking.

"Wow. What's *her* problem?" Josh asked as we started up the steps again.

I cleared my throat, my stomach feeling suddenly queasy. Missy hadn't spoken to me once in the three months since my birthday, when Mrs. Kane held us all hostage, but it didn't bother me. Everyone dealt with having their lives endangered in a different way, and it wasn't as if we'd ever been real friends. But I'd never thought I could feel threatened by her. Until now.

"I don't know," I said warily.

Josh and I both paused. We'd just arrived at the top floor and could hear angry voices coming from the back office. From Headmaster Hathaway's office.

". . . why you can't do something about it!"

"Contrary to popular belief, Sawyer, I'm not all-powerful."

"I don't even understand why we're talking about this. This whole thing is completely stupid."

"Was that Graham?" I whispered to Josh.

He nodded. "And Sawyer."

We hesitated at the threshold of the outer office—the one usually occupied by Headmaster Hathaway's assistant. Right now the large, airy waiting area was empty, the computer screen atop the wide oak desk blank, the rolling chair tucked in.

"What should we do?" I asked Josh.

"I say we knock before they find us out here frozen like a couple of eavesdroppers," he replied.

"Good plan."

We crossed the room and Josh banged loudly on the door. Instantly the voices fell silent. The door swung open and the Headmaster stood there, his light green tie slightly loosened. He wore no jacket, and his expression was both frazzled and impatient.

"Hello, Miss Brennan," he said to me. Then his eyes flicked dismissively to Josh. "Mr. Hollis."

Graham shoved past his father, shot Josh a look that was obviously meant to kill, and kept walking without a word. There was no love lost between Graham and Josh. A couple of years earlier, Josh had dated and broken up with Graham's twin sister, Jen, who had tragically taken her own life soon afterward. Graham held some kind of grudge against Josh over the whole thing, and from the way Mr. Hathaway was coldly staring Josh down, I wondered if he did too.

"Sawyer, Josh," Mr. Hathaway said, folding his arms over his chest. "If you would kindly excuse us."

Sawyer, who had become one of my best friends over the past few months, ducked his head so that his blond hair fell over his eyes, and slipped past his dad. As he walked by me, he mouthed the words, "I tried." And then he was gone. A skittering sense of foreboding shot right through me.

"I'll wait for you downstairs," Josh whispered.

Then he shut the door behind him, and I found myself alone with the headmaster. His office was bright and sunny, the large windows thrown open to let in the fresh spring air. The heavy curtains billowed, then slapped against the molding as the wind died down. Mr. Hathaway gestured at the chair across from his desk, and I sat. He sighed, shoved his hands through his light brown hair, and lowered himself down in the seat across from mine. As he laced his fingers together atop his leather desk blotter, I realized that, for the first time since I'd know him, he looked slightly older than his forty-some-odd years.

"I'm truly sorry to have to tell you this, Reed, but it looks like the ribbon-cutting ceremony you were expecting to have this weekend will have to be postponed," he said, not sounding sorry at all. "Indefinitely."

My heart dropped all the way through the floor, probably landing somewhere near Josh's feet four stories below. No. No, no, no, no, no. Hundreds of alumnae were flying in for this event from all over the world. I had alerted the press. I had hired a caterer and ordered fifty bottles of seriously expensive champagne. I'd laid out all that cash for the cocktail party on Saturday night, for the hotel rooms, for the Sunday morning brunch. If I called it off now, I was going to look like a clueless little kid. And the new Billings would be pegged as a failure before the first stone was laid.

"Why?" was all I could manage to say.

"Unfortunately, it seems that the plans you submitted are not up to code," the headmaster said, looking me in the eye. "There's a new green initiative in the county, and unless the plans are changed significantly, the zoning board is going to kill the project entirely."

My fingers curled around the leather armrests on my chair. "What? But the town approved the plans," I said, my voice pitching itself up in a panic.

"I know, but now someone has submitted them to the county," he said slowly, as if speaking to a chimpanzee.

"Who?" I said. "Why?"

I kind of sounded like a chimpanzee, actually. I cleared my throat and tried to get my thoughts in order, but none of this made sense and all I could think was that this wasn't fair. It just wasn't fair. At that moment my phone rang, and I felt like I was going to explode out of my skin. I reached into my bag and pressed down on the ignore button as hard as I could. Janice Winthrop wasn't going to care much about which suite she was booked in when she found out there was no longer an event to attend.

"I don't know," the headmaster said. He tugged a piece of paper toward him and tilted it up to read. "But apparently the plans need to include the following: fifty percent sustainable materials; energy-efficient lighting, heating, and plumbing; and a solar panel to help ease the carbon footprint. Which, apparently, will at least get us a tax break from the state."

"Oh my God." I slumped back in my chair and my fingers automatically fluttered up to touch the locket. The current plans for the new Billings did include some green materials and plans for energy-efficient appliances and light fixtures, but I didn't recall anything about heating and plumbing, and no one had ever mentioned a solar panel. "What am I going to do?"

"I don't know, Miss Brennan," he said. He tugged out another copy of the letter from the county and handed it to me. "But considering all the difficulties we've had on campus lately, I can't go up against the county right now. So until you figure this out with your design team, the Billings project is officially shelved."

THE NEW MISSY

"I don't get it," Constance Talbot said. Sun shone through the skylight at the center of the Easton dining hall, turning her red hair golden. "Who could have sent the plans to the county? We're the only ones who have seen them."

Around the table, my Billings friends wore varying expressions of concern, suspicion, and disappointment. Normally we took up two tables in the cafeteria, but for the moment, every last one of us was gathered around one table, and they were all leaning in over one another so they could hear my story. Even London Simmons and Shelby Wordsworth were there. After the insanity that had occurred on my birthday, we had all voted and decided to relax the rules that governed the Billings Literary Society—the secret club that I had started back in January. In fact, we'd kind of abandoned the thing entirely, giving up on the midnight meetings in the Billings Chapel and all the crazy talk of witchcraft. It just hadn't seemed right to go back there, after all the terror and misery the BLS and the book of spells had brought us. And although I knew that Kiki Rosen was still experimenting with some spells on her own, the rest of us hadn't dabbled at all, content to try to get things back to normal. Which also meant that London, Shelby, and Constance had been hanging out with us again. Everyone was back together. Well, everyone except for Missy.

"Actually, that's not exactly true," I said, leaning back in my wooden chair at the head of the table and tucking my brown hair behind my ears. "My architect and contractors have them, of course—"

"But none of them would send them to the county if they knew it meant getting shut down," Tiffany Goulborne pointed out. "They'd be out of a job."

"True," I conceded. "But I also sent them to some of the wealthier alumnae."

"WTF? Why did you do that?" Portia Ahronian said, clutching the dozen gold necklaces around her neck. "You have enough money to build this thing ten times over."

"I know, but I thought it would be nice to get other people involved," I said. "The more they feel like part of the new Billings, the more they'll be invested in its future."

"She's right, you guys. We need the alums," Rose Sakowitz said, looking around at the others. She looked even tinier and more adorable than usual in a pink plaid sundress with her red curls held back by a tortoiseshell band. "Think of how many times they've supported us when things have gone . . ." She trailed off.

"I think 'awry' is the word you're looking for," Tiffany put in, shifting in her seat. "Like when Cheyenne . . . passed away and we had to elect a new president? They don't usually have to come up with two presidential gifts in one year."

I squirmed a bit, recalling the amount of cash and all the expensive presents that had been dropped in my lap after I'd been elected in the fall—not to mention the very thorough and useful files on the current Billings Girls and our alums that I'd been gifted.

"And how Suzel told us about the secret passage at Gwendolyn so we could get to the Legacy last semester?" London added, clicking a rhinestone-encrusted compact closed after checking her lipstick. "She's, like, a total asset."

"Seriously," Shelby said, checking the end of her dark blond braid for split ends. "The alumnae have been keeping us afloat for years."

"Yeah, but after everything that's happened, can we really trust any of them?" Astrid Chou said as she reorganized her paintbrushes inside a funky, polka-dotted carrying case. "I mean, if this was three months ago, you probably would have sent the plans to Cheyenne's batty mother."

I swallowed hard, my eyes flicking to Noelle. She was the only one not participating in the conversation, choosing instead to sit at the far end of the table and page through *Vogue*. My phone beeped loudly.

"Is your phone possessed or what?" Amberly Carmichael asked, pressing the palms of her perfectly manicured hands into the edge of the table. "It hasn't stopped since we got here."

I groaned, pulling my phone out to silence it. "Sorry."

Astrid did, of course, have a point. I always thought Cheyenne's mom, Mrs. Martin, was a cool woman, someone who loved Billings and would have done anything for us. Until I found out she believed in this hundred-year-old curse and thought that five of my friends and I needed to die in order to break it.

"I don't know, you guys. Most of the people I sent the plans to seemed really excited. Some of them even donated money," I told them. "I can't imagine that any of them would have wanted to sabotage the project."

Everyone around the table exchanged wary glances, as if waiting for one of us to confess. Finally Kiki Rosen leaned forward, wrapping her earbud wires around her iPod before she shoved it into her battered canvas backpack.

"Okay. Forget who screwed us. The real question is, how do we get unscrewed?" she asked.

"We have to go back to the drawing board. Literally," I said with a sigh. "I already spoke to my architect and she said she could modify the plans, but since a lot of the materials have already been ordered, it's going to cost a lot more money. Plus it takes a while to get some of these green materials, so that will cause some serious delays."

"How serious?" Amberly asked.

I licked my lips, dreading what I had to say next. My phone rang again. One more ignore. "Billings might not be ready by the fall. It might not even be ready until the *following* fall."

"What?" Lorna Gross gasped, her dark brown eyes wide. "But most of us will be gone by then."

"Everyone but Amberly," I said flatly.

"This sucks," Astrid said, shoving a potato chip into her mouth.

"Tell me about it," I replied.

Suddenly, Lorna sat up straight and leaned back, out into the aisle. "Hey, Missy!" she called out loudly, giving a wave.

I turned around to see Missy Thurber striding right by our table, her wide-nostriled nose in the air as she completely ignored us. Her French braid swung haughtily down the center of her back, and she didn't even blink when she heard her former best friend calling out to her.

This was the new Missy. It wasn't just me she'd been ignoring. She had stopped returning any and all calls from the Billings crew, had stopped saying hello to us in the hallways, had stopped even looking in our direction, unless it was to shoot me evil glares. It was like all of us, and everything we'd been through together, had been excised from her brain.

"That girl puts the 'lone' in 'loner,'" Vienna said, rolling her eyes.

Instead of turning toward the small corner table she'd been occupying by herself for every meal since March, she hooked a left and walked right over to a table full of guys. Senior guys. Popular senior guys and a few of their female hangers-on. Graham Hathaway greeted her with a smile and made a big show of pulling out a chair for her. Missy sat with a self-satisfied twist of her lips. Then Graham ran off to the food line to get her lunch.

"Since when are those two BFF?" Portia asked, clearly annoyed.

I glanced over my shoulder at the table where Josh; his roommate,

Trey Prescott; and some of his other friends were sitting, and saw that they had noticed Missy and Graham as well. Josh and Trey, in particular, shot Graham annoyed looks as he returned seconds later with a bagel sandwich and iced tea for Missy. I sat back hard in my chair and slumped.

Call me crazy, but the idea of my worst enemy at Easton and Josh's worst enemy at Easton hanging out together made my blood run cold.

I sat in my final class of the day that afternoon, staring out across the quad at the now-silent construction zone. The bulldozers and the backhoe sat motionless in the center of the plot, as if their drivers had up and fled right in the middle of work. It made them look oddly lonely and sad, like great, hulking orphans. Up at the front of the classroom, Mr. Cheever helpfully outlined every item that would be on my calculus final, but I hadn't once looked up at the board. Instead, my eyes were trained on that damn frozen backhoe, as if simply glaring at it would make it roar to life.

I had already placed calls to every important county executive I could find online, not knowing which one might be able to help me, but it wasn't like it mattered. I'd been screened by each of their assistants and no one had called me back. I wished Mr. Lange were still alive. He would have known exactly the right person to contact, exactly how to smooth things over. But me? I was clueless and utterly lost. And I didn't like the feeling.

I could have gotten in touch with Chester Worth again, but I tried not to bother him too much. Sometimes I could tell that the tentative phone calls of a naive schoolgirl grated on his nerves, almost as much as the tenth call of the day from Janice Winthrop grated on mine, and just knowing that I might be annoying him made me nervous to call. Somewhere in the back of both our minds, we realized I was not his responsibility, and sooner or later his duty to his deceased business partner was going to wear out.

If only I could get Noelle involved. That girl was definitely her father's daughter. It was like she instinctively knew how to get things done, and get them done right. She had a way of talking to people that made them snap to attention.

But Noelle was off the project and, deep down, I knew why. She was angry at me because that knife her father had taken in the gut had been meant for me. She had never said it, she probably never would, but I knew she was thinking it. She had to be. Because I was thinking it too. I'd been thinking it every day since it happened, feeling the weight of it, the crushing blame. Our father had died to save me. I spent at least 99 percent of my waking hours trying not to let that fact overwhelm me. Which was another reason that rebuilding Billings was so important to me. Staying focused on every minute detail of such an overwhelming project kept me from obsessing on other, more horrifying thoughts.

I knew Noelle wouldn't have wanted to lose me, but I often wondered, if it had come down to a choice between me and her father, which one of us would she have chosen to keep alive?

Someone in the room coughed, rousing me from my thoughts. I

looked at the board and quickly jotted down a few notes, but there was no way I could catch up now. I glanced across the two rows of diligent students that separated me from Sawyer and hoped that he was taking good notes, because I was definitely going to need to borrow them.

Suddenly, I saw something flash out by the construction site. Someone was walking quickly away from one of the trailers. It didn't look like one of the workers, though. He was too slim, too skittish, too young. He wore a black canvas jacket and a baseball cap and was moving so fast and furtively it made my nerves sizzle.

My phone vibrated in the back pocket of my jeans, making me jump. Behind me, Astrid snorted a laugh. I yanked the phone out and held it in both hands under my desk, cursing whichever alumna had decided to scare the crap out of me in the middle of class. The text was from an unknown number. Even though this wasn't completely out of the ordinary—some of the alums had texted from numbers I didn't have stored in my phone—my heart still pitter-pattered nervously. I'd had some bad luck with mystery texts in my recent past when Noelle and her grandmother had staged her fake kidnapping and sent me on a series of ridiculous tasks to get her back.

At the board Mr. Cheever droned on. I held my breath and opened the text.

U KNO U'VE GOT POWERFL ALUMS ON UR SIDE W/BILLINGS. U JUST NEED 2 FIND RIGHT ONE. HINT: SHE'S FILED UNDER G.

My throat went dry. I glanced around the classroom, but everyone in sight was focused on the teacher, their pens scratching over
their notebooks. No one had a phone out—not Missy, not Lorna,
not Diana Waters, not Sawyer or Marc Alberro. Of course, not every
student at Easton was in this classroom, but most of them were currently in class somewhere. And technically, texting in class was
verboten. But anyone could have sent this message and then stashed
their phone away before I even had a chance to pull my cell out of my
pocket.

My fingers trembling, I texted back.

WHO R U?

The message came up that it was sending. And sending. And sending. Then the screen lit up with the words: MSG FAILED.

Pressing my teeth together in frustration, I tried again.

WHO R U?

MSG FAILED.

I sat back hard in my chair and turned my phone off, mentally letting out a string of curses that, if spoken aloud, would have landed me
in detention for a week.

Then, out in the hallway, I heard a giggle. I glanced up at the open
door just as someone darted past. A blond someone in a pink dress.
My heart completely seized and I sat up straight, but no one else in the

room seemed to have noticed. It was all I could do to keep myself from sprinting across the room and checking the hall.

I glanced around the desks again, and my eyes met Missy's. She was glaring at me from across two rows of desks, her mouth set in an angry red line.

"Reed," Astrid whispered from behind me. "Are you all right?"

"Yeah. I'm fine," I whispered back hoarsely, tearing my gaze away from Missy's to face forward again.

My hands trembled beneath my desk, holding tight to my phone. I felt vulnerable and small, as if at any moment someone or something was about to attack. But the hallway was silent now, and the construction site was still, nothing moving other than the flag atop the crane, flapping in the breeze.

MT

"You've been stalked more this year than half the starlets in Hollywood combined. I'm not sure whether to be proud, jealous, or just seriously disturbed."

Ivy Slade handed my phone back to me after reading my mystery text and arched one perfectly plucked eyebrow. She stood in the center of my single dorm room in Pemberly Hall with her slim arms crossed over her chest. Her dark hair hung loose over the shoulders of her white cardigan, and she looked as if she'd been spray-painted into her dark-wash skinny jeans.

"Believe me, it's not something I'm proud of," I told her, tossing my phone onto my bed. I glanced out the window toward the construction site, checking for dark-jacketed creepers or random girls with blond hair. "So what do I do now?"

"How much time do you have before Josh comes to pick you up?" she asked, sliding past me to sit at my desk. She opened my laptop and the screen instantly filled with at least ten open documents—outlines of my plans for the cocktail party and brunch; contact numbers for caterers, car services, florists, and hotels; guest lists; meal preferences; and arrival times. Just looking it was giving me a migraine.

"About ten minutes," I replied, checking my watch. Josh had been busy most of the day, but we'd had a standing predinner coffee date for weeks now. So standard that all my friends knew I basically planned my day around it. It was the best and most chill part of my day. "What are you thinking?"

"I'm thinking we start by checking to see if this stalker's info is any good," Ivy said, tossing her hair over her shoulder as she looked back at me. I was already staring out the window again. "Hello? Can I have your attention, please?"

With a sigh I yanked the curtain over the window and then sat down on the edge of my bed. "Can we *not* call it a stalker? Just hearing the word gives me the heebs."

Ivy's red lips twisted into a smirk. "Fine. Mystery texter it is. MT for short."

I smiled as Ivy opened the most valuable folder on my computer—the one containing all the information there was to know about every last Billings alum and all the current Billings Girls as well. There were several files, each with the information organized in different ways—by class, by initiation date, by last name. Ivy opened the alphabetical file and went right for the G's.

"So. What are we looking for?" Ivy asked.

"I have no idea." I wiped my sweaty palms on my thighs and

scooted forward a bit. "Someone in county government? Or state?"

Ivy clicked on the first *G* name, Lacey Galvin, but apparently Lacey was a world-class yachtswoman living in Florida. She closed the file and opened the next.

"Or maybe someone in construction?" she said. "Green living?"

The next woman owned five hotels in France. The next was listed as a life coach in Los Angeles. There was an Olympic equestrian, a CEO of a gourmet food corporation, and several philanthropists, but no one working on environmental causes. By the time we got to the last woman in the *G* section, Cori Gulberg, I was starting to think that this MT person was either out of their minds, or so bored they were making stuff up for fun.

"Here's something," Ivy said, snagging my attention. "Cori Gulberg is president of Glace Cosmetics."

I turned up my palms. "So?"

"It says they're leaders in green initiatives in their field," Ivy said, though even she sounded skeptical.

"They make organic blush and primer. That's gonna be really helpful," I groused, pushing myself up. I shooed her out of my chair. "Get up. Go!"

"Why? We're done with the G's. What do you think you're going to find that I didn't?" Ivy complained. She finally stood up when she saw that I was about to sit down on her lap.

"I don't know," I said. "There has to be something."

I started scrolling through the entire alphabetical list, as if I was going to find some *G* name misfiled under *M*.

"No, actually there doesn't," Ivy said, hovering over me. "It looks like our little MT just felt like sending you on a pointless mission."

"But why?" I asked, tearing my eyes from the screen as random names flew by faster and faster and faster. "Why bother? Just so that we'd waste a few minutes on my laptop?"

Suddenly, Ivy's eyes widened at the computer screen. "Wait! Stop! Go back."

I lifted my fingers from the touchpad. "Go back where?"

"To the *S* section," she said, shaking her finger at the screen in frustration. "Did I just see the name Carolina Slavowski?"

"Um . . . maybe." I scrolled back. What someone with the initials *CS* had to do with *G* was beyond me, but Ivy was acting like a puppy dog that had just spotted its first cat. I found the name Carolina Slavowski and hovered the arrow over it.

"And we're interested in this person why?"

"Carolina Slavowski is the real name of Carolina Grant."

I stared at Ivy blankly. "Who the hell is Carolina Grant?"

"From Renovate TV?" Ivy prodded me. She rolled her eyes at my continued dumb stare. "She does all these green renovations, over-hauling houses to reduce their carbon footprint, helping businesses get up to code . . ." She clucked her tongue and nudged me aside with her shoulder, angling for the keyboard. "Here."

It took two seconds for her to bring up the Renovate TV website and toggle to a show called *Go Green!* Suddenly a video popped up on the screen, featuring a bright-eyed, curly-haired woman who was spunk personified.

"Hi! I'm Carolina Grant!" she said as she walked along a pristine beach in jeans, a T-shirt, and a tool belt. "Do you want to have the greenest, most cost-efficient, most Earth-friendly home on *your* block? We're looking for new homes to renovate for next season's episodes of *Go Green!* Simply click on the link to my left and fill out the entry form. You could be the next person to join the Go Green revolution!"

The video stopped and I gaped at Ivy. "She went to Easton?"

"That just makes her so much more awesome," Ivy said reverently.

I leaned back, narrowing my eyes at her. "You watch Renovate TV?"

Ivy crossed her arms over her chest and stood up straight. "Sex addicts need sex. Drug addicts need drugs. I need to watch people demolish their homes and rebuild them again. Got a problem with that?"

I laughed. "Just seeing a whole new side of you, that's all."

"You do realize what this means, right?" Ivy said, grabbing my phone up off my bed. "It means that your MT is on the up and up."

I turned around and stared at Carolina Grant's frozen made-for-TV smile. "And it also means that we may have just found somebody who could help us fast-track Billings."

Suddenly, I felt as if a huge weight was being lifted off my heart, and I found myself sitting up a little straighter. Maybe this project didn't have to be shelved after all. Maybe there was something I could do to fix it. Who needed Noelle when I could have Carolina Grant?

"Thank you, MT," I said under my breath.

"Should we call her?" Ivy asked, practically hyperventilating as she clutched my cell. Clearly the idea of talking to Carolina was making her dizzy.

"Definitely," I said.

And then my stomach grumbled. My eyes darted to the clock on my desk and I frowned. Embroiled in our research, I'd lost track of time, and Josh was over twenty minutes late.

"Can I have my phone? I just need to call Josh real quick."

Ivy's smile drooped, but she handed the phone over. "Sure."

It took four rings for Josh to pick up. "Reed, hey," he whispered.

"Hey," I said. "I just wanted to make sure you were all right. We still on for coffee?"

I was kind of dying to see him, especially now. I wanted to tell him about MT and the helpful info he or she had helped us dig up. Although, knowing Josh, he'd probably tell me to block MT's number and never think about it again. He was decidedly anti-intrigue. And for good reason, considering our track record.

"You can't go out now! What about calling Carolina?" Ivy hissed, nudging my arm. I batted her hand away.

"Crap, I'm so sorry," Josh said. His voice got gradually louder until he was speaking normally. "I totally spaced. Trey got us passes to go off campus for pizza, so I'm not gonna be back for a while."

My heart thumped extra hard. He'd spaced on our standing date? That was very not like him.

"Um, okay," I said, trying to sound upbeat. "It's no big deal. I've got a lot to do anyway."

"You sure?" Josh asked. I heard a horn honk in the background and assumed he was standing outside the pizza place now. But why couldn't he talk to me in front of Trey? Why had he been whispering when he'd picked up?

"Sure," I said, forcing a smile. "Call me later?"

"I will," he said. "I love you."

"Love you, too," I replied.

Then the line went dead. I sat and stared at the phone until the screen went dark. I had this hot, roiling feeling in my gut. Something had been off with that phone call.

"He's not coming?" Ivy asked.

"Apparently not," I replied.

"Good. That means we can call Carolina now!"

She snatched the phone out of my hand and leaned toward the computer to reopen Carolina's file and get her cell number—far more efficient than filling out the cable TV station's online form. I rolled my eyes, but got up to give her more space. My heart felt heavy and twisted in knots thanks to Josh's careless disregard of our date, but I told myself it was actually a good thing. Now I could get right on this Billings problem. Really, his sudden and unexpected thoughtlessness was a blessing in disguise.

Right?

THE POWER

"I was so excited when I hung up the phone with you, you have no idea," Carolina Grant gushed as she walked at an inhuman speed from the parking circle, down the pathway between Bradwell and Pemberly, and toward the quad. Her crew scurried after her—one woman with a headset and an iPad, a guy with a smallish camera, and another toting a ridiculously large microphone over her head. "I haven't been back here since . . . oh my God, I'm too embarrassed to say when I actually graduated, but let's just say it's been a *long* time."

"Well, I'm glad you could make it on such short notice." We had only called Carolina last night, and less than eighteen hours later, here she was, ready to get to work and save my butt. I guess Billings connections really did mean something.

Thank you, MT, I thought, somewhat grudgingly. The very idea that I owed my new luck to some freak who felt the need to text me anonymously made my skin prickle.

"So glad," Ivy echoed, an admiring gleam in her dark eyes.

"I sent you an invite to the ribbon-cutting festivities this weekend, but it came back to me as undeliverable," I told her. After our phone call the night before, I'd double-checked my guest-list records and discovered the mistake, which, of course, made me feel somehow totally rude and incompetent. "Otherwise you would have known about this sooner."

"Oh, that happens all the time, since I'm constantly changing my e-mail to avoid crazed fans," Carolina said, waving a dismissive hand. She stopped short as she emerged onto the open green space at the center of the Easton campus. "Oh. My. God. *Nothing* has changed!"

She clasped her hands together in front of her chest and I glanced over at Ivy, who had never been a fan of overenthusiasm. Sometimes when she was around Constance I got the awful feeling she was going to haul off and punch the girl in the face just for being her natural bubbly self. Now I expected a good eye roll at the very least, but instead she looked . . . giddy. I guess, like she'd said last night, we all had our things. Then Carolina's gaze fell on the still dormant construction site and her smile completely disappeared.

"Well. Except for that." She whipped around and looked at the camera. "Christopher? Can you get a good shot of that? That is where my dorm, Billings, used to be."

"You got it, CG," Christopher replied, bringing the camera to his shoulder. "And we're rolling."

Carolina took my arm and steered me down one of the stone pathways toward the Billings site, holding me close to her side as Ivy scurried to keep up. She wore a blue-and-white plaid shirt with snap buttons and destroyed designer jeans. Her thick hair smelled of apricots and, now that I was close up, I could see that she had on tons of makeup to hide what appeared to be acne scars. It was kind of nice to know that someone so beautiful and famous still had a few flaws to deal with.

"Now just act natural," she said under her breath. "This is all just for the B roll. Establishing shots. Stuff like that."

"Okay."

All around us, people dropped what they were doing and turned to stare. A group of freshmen seated in a study circle looked up from their laptops and pointed. Trey and Gage Coolidge stopped tossing around a football and eyed us curiously. Even a group of teachers over by the Hell Hall stairs paused to gape. Suddenly it wasn't the camera I was worried about. It was all the attention.

"Ugh. I was so disgusted and sad when I heard they had torn this place down," Carolina said. "Now that I see it, I'm just plain depressed."

We had come to the edge of the construction site, and she stared down at the spot where the front steps had once stood—a small area still untouched by the construction. You could still make out the indent where the bottom stone stair used to be, and she traced the corner of it with the toe of her work boot.

"This place really was like a second home," she said, staring wistfully up at the sky. Christopher zoomed in on her as the microphone guy hovered the fuzzy boom over her head. Her expression was nostalgic and morose. "I'm honored that I'll have the chance to rebuild it," she said reverently. Then she looked directly into the lens and brightened like a firework lighting the night sky. "In true green fashion, of course!"

Ivy clapped quietly and I tried not to laugh. As Carolina began to walk the perimeter, dragging her crew and her superfan with her, I gazed across at the trailers and narrowed my eyes. Was that creepy figure yesterday just a curious student checking things out, or had he been here for a more sinister reason? Fingering Eliza Williams's locket, I was about to walk over and check things out when I got that eerie, skin-tingling feeling that I was being watched. I turned around quickly, half expecting to see a mysterious blond girl staring me down, and was surprised to find Noelle standing under a tree about fifty yards off. Her arms were clutched around her stomach, and her sunglasses covered half her face. I smiled and waved her over, hoping that meeting Carolina might perk her up, but she acted as if she hadn't even seen me. She slipped her phone out of her bag and ducked her head to talk as she walked off in the opposite direction. My heart thumped with this odd, disappointed foreboding, and again my skin started to prickle. This was never going to feel right if Noelle couldn't get behind it.

"Now here's what I'm thinking." Carolina flung her arms out wide as if getting ready to paint a picture of her vision. "The taller the building, the—"

"Excuse me! Excuse me! Miss Brennan!"

We all turned around to watch as the headmaster speed-walked toward us across the quad, not even bothering to use the pathways. Missy and her cousin Paige Ryan scurried after him, like his personal and very alert assistants, which made my stomach turn. Paige and Missy had been involved in the previous plan to rebuild Billings— the one that had also included several of the women who had helped orchestrate and execute my latest near-death experience and Mr. Lange's murder. Which, of course, made me wonder what the hell they were doing here now, and why they appeared to be so buddy-buddy with the headmaster.

Headmaster Hathaway tried to get his breathing under control as he arrived in front of us. He shot the camera a scathing look.

"Would you mind turning that thing off?"

Christopher didn't move.

"Sorry. He's under strict orders to only answer to me," Carolina said with a wide grin. She offered the headmaster her hand. "I'm Carolina Grant of *Go Green!*, the number-one show on Renovate TV. And you are?"

"I'm William Hathaway. Headmaster of Easton Academy," he replied, quickly grasping her hand. "Now what is the meaning of all of this?"

"Headmaster? Fantastic!" Carolina blurted, clasping her hands. "Then you and I are going to be spending a lot of time together. Reed here has asked me to oversee the reconstruction of Billings House, ensuring that it meets all the green standards of the county, but we're going to do much more than that, aren't we, Reed?"

I blinked. Her grin was practically blinding.

"We're going to exceed those standards!" Carolina announced, putting her arm around the headmaster's back.

Headmaster Hathaway went as stiff as a board. I'd never seen him look so uncomfortable.

"I thought the project was shelved," Paige said in a snide tone, looking me up and down. "Isn't that what you told us, Mr. Hathaway?"

My fingers curled into fists. Why was she even here? And what was the headmaster doing discussing the status of my project with her? Then, just like that, it hit me. It hit me so hard my brain felt suddenly weightless. Maybe Missy and Paige had sent the plans to the county. They definitely had the motive—they wanted more than anything to keep me from rebuilding Billings my way. But how had they gotten hold of the plans?

Headmaster Hathaway extricated himself from Carolina's grasp and scratched just above his eyebrow. "Yes, well, from what I understood, it was going to take months for Miss Brennan's contractors to acquire the green supplies required to—"

"Please. Nothing takes months once I get involved!" Carolina said. "I have connections at every major green company in the country. I can have every little thing we need delivered here like that!" she said, snapping her fingers.

Frown lines creased the headmaster's forehead. "I appreciate your good intentions, Miss Grant, but the truth of the matter is that it's not that simple," he said. "This sort of thing must be voted on by the board of directors. Having a camera crew on campus is a serious privacy issue," he added, glancing at the camera lens as Christopher zoomed in. He straightened his jacket and cleared his throat. "Each and every one of our students and faculty will need to sign waivers. There are permits to procure . . ."

With each new objection, my hope deflated further and further until it was nothing but a tiny, wrinkled, airless balloon. I had thought that Headmaster Hathaway had finally come around to being on my side—at least he'd attempted to act disappointed when he'd told me about the county's restrictions. But now, I had to wonder. Had he been psyched to get that letter from the county? Was he relieved to have a reason to shut me down and blame someone else? I knew he'd never been a fan of Billings—it had been his idea to raze it in the first place—but after I'd donated all that money I thought he'd pretty much jumped on board the Reed train. Apparently not so much.

As Hathaway continued his point-by-point case, Carolina put on a pensive expression and nodded thoughtfully. She shot me a quick glance, clearly prodding me to say something, and panic welled up inside my chest. What was I supposed to say? They were the adults here. I was just a student. And besides, how was I supposed to know how to deal with privacy waivers and consent forms? Did I look like I'd graduated from law school recently?

"Of course, of course," Carolina said, finally realizing I was going to remain mute. She cast a glance over her shoulder at iPad girl. "And when is the next board meeting?"

"Well . . . this Thursday night," the headmaster said. "But I'm sure there's no way you can be prepared in time to—"

She nodded at her assistant, who tapped her iPad's screen. "We'll be there."

My jaw dropped slightly. Was she serious? She was still committed after hearing all that?

Double H stared at her for a moment, dumbfounded as well. For once we were on the same page. "You'll be there."

"Yes. We'll be there. We'll present our plans and answer any concerns your board may have," Carolina said definitively. Then the smile was back on again. "I look forward to working with you, Mr. Hathaway!"

The headmaster clicked his teeth together. Clearly the frustration over not having a comeback was killing him. And I was loving every minute of it. I wanted to turn around and kiss Carolina. Calling her in had been the best idea ever.

"See you then," the headmaster muttered finally. He turned and walked away, retracing his steps through the freshly clipped grass toward Hell Hall. I shot Missy and Paige a triumphant look and they both rolled their eyes at me before following Double H. As they stormed off, I could have sworn I heard Missy let out a growling sort of groan. Apparently the frustration was contagious.

"Well," Ivy said. "That was fun."

"Why didn't you say anything, Reed? This is your baby," Carolina asked, grasping my shoulder.

"I don't . . . I mean, you seemed to have it under control, so—"

"Yes, but you're the one in charge. You're the face of the project," Carolina said in a pep-talky way. "If you can't defend it, no one can.

Or should, for that matter. If a leader doesn't believe in her own cause, what's the point?"

I swallowed. It was the quickest plummet of all time from victorious to humiliated, guilty, and unworthy. "I'm sorry."

"Don't be sorry. Start sticking up for yourself!" Ivy said, jumping on Carolina's bandwagon.

Carolina put both hands on my shoulders, forcing me to look her in the eye.

"Money means power, Reed. You've got all the power here. Sure, my fame is going to help speed up the process, but you're the one who got us this far. You can't let a little grandstanding like that stop you," she added, chucking her chin toward the retreating headmaster. "If you do, then you are *not* your father's daughter."

Just like that, my shoulder muscles coiled. How did she even know who my biological father was? But then . . . maybe she did have a point. My hand fluttered up and touched my locket. Maybe it was time to start accepting, or even embracing, the fact that I had Lange blood in my veins. I'd been through a lot in the past couple of years. I was a seriously strong person, right? I didn't need Mr. Lange or Noelle to speak for me. I could speak for myself.

"So, are you in or are you out?" Carolina asked me, releasing me finally and standing up straight.

I smiled slowly, my own posture lengthening as the sun warmed my face. "I'm in."

PEACEFUL PERFECTION

Later, just as the sun was starting to go down, Josh and I comman-
deered a couch near the window wall of the solarium, cuddling back
against one of the arms with our legs up on the cushions. The large,
airy room was jam-packed with students, and we caught more than a
few annoyed looks as underclassmen searched for empty seats, but I
didn't care. In a few weeks Josh would be graduating. Each moment
like this one was precious. Besides, he was a senior and seniors could
pretty much do what they wanted around school these days. A perk of
being basically outta there.

"What was I thinking last night?" Josh said into my hair. "No pizza
is good enough to make me miss this."

"Yep. Pretty dumb move if you ask me." I smiled, turning to the side
so I could see him better. I felt a pang when I saw the guilt written all
over his face. "I'm just kidding. It's okay. It was just one date. Actually, it
wasn't even a date, it was a hang. You missed one datelike hang. No big."

Surprisingly, I realized I actually meant what I was saying. Josh had told me he was sorry so many times over the past twenty-four hours that *I* was starting to feel guilty for being annoyed about it in the first place—not to mention more than a little clingy. Couldn't the guy go out for food with his friends without me getting all jealous about it? I wasn't the only one he was leaving behind when he went off to school. Pretty soon the guys he hung out with every day wouldn't be there. Every time I thought about not seeing Noelle and Ivy every day, it made my spirits sink.

"One datelike hang too many," Josh said under his breath.

He leaned down to kiss me and I looped my arms up and around his neck. We half-lay there like that and kissed and kissed and kissed until I forgot we were in the middle of a crowded room.

"Yeah! Take it *all* off!" Gage Coolidge shouted at us.

Josh and I broke apart and a bunch of people applauded, hooting and hollering and shouting more gross crap—enough to make me blush. I glanced at Josh sheepishly. Oops.

"I think we're making people sick," Josh said with a smirk. "Or possibly turning them on."

"Either way, not my problem," I said, even though my skin was on fire.

I leaned back into the crook of his arm again and sighed happily. This was definitely the most perfect moment of my week so far. I was not going to think about Billings or Thursday's board meeting or what the future might hold for me and Josh. I wasn't even going to think about MT, about whom Josh was still in the dark. I wanted to tell him, but after the awesome meeting with Carolina that afternoon, the last thing I wanted was a lecture about how I shouldn't trust anonymous texters. I'd get around to telling him eventually. Just . . . not tonight.

Tonight I was just going to sit here and think about this. About us. About how his arm was warm on top of mine, how I could hear his heartbeat through his polo shirt, how he smelled of evergreen soap and paint and cherry lollipop.

Lazily, happily, my eyes scanned the room full of students, none of whom could possibly have any clue what it felt like to be as content as I was at that very moment. Some of them gazed at us dreamily, others were oblivious to my existence, and some, like Gage, were still mocking us from afar. But I didn't care. Everything was utterly peaceful and perfect.

Until suddenly, abruptly, my eyes fell on Graham Hathaway.

He stood diagonally across the room, alone, and he was staring right at me. Glaring, really. His hands were tucked under the lapels of his suede jacket and he had dark circles under his eyes, as if he either hadn't slept in days or had suddenly discovered hard drugs. He held my gaze and kept right on glowering until my heart felt like it was going to pound out of my chest.

But what the hell was his problem?

Then Missy and Paige walked over to him from the Coffee Carma counter, and Missy handed him a coffee. All the little hairs on the back of my neck stood on end. Paige was *still* on campus. And now the gruesome twosome from lunch yesterday had morphed into a gruesome threesome.

"What's she doing here?" Josh asked, following my gaze.

"Who knows," I said, trying to sound casual. "I'm starting to think she has no life."

Graham chatted with the two girls happily as they sipped their drinks. Just like that he was back to being smiling, jovial Graham. He pointed to a table being vacated by a klatch of teachers, and the three of them made a beeline for the coveted seats. I watched them for a while as my pulse began to cool, wondering if I'd just imagined it. Wondering if he'd look my way again.

But he never did. And before long I found myself thinking I'd somehow imagined the whole thing.

THE TIDE

Headmaster Hathaway was starting to squirm. Clearly I'd been right about him not wanting Billings rebuilt after all, because as soon as things started to sort of swing my way at the board meeting, he'd begun clearing his throat at odd intervals and he kept shifting his weight in his chair, making it squeak and squeal.

Oh well, I thought, feeling betrayed as I watched him tap his pen against the long table behind which he and the rest of the board members sat. *Sucks to be you.*

When we'd first arrived, my hopes had not been high. Probably because the first people I'd seen upon entering the Great Room at Mitchell Hall were Missy, Paige, and her twin brother, Daniel, who appeared to have gathered an anti-rebuilding contingent near the front row. Plus, even though most of the student body was present, gathered behind me in chairs and along the walls of the room, neither Josh nor Noelle was there. Josh had told me he'd be stuck at the library finishing a paper, and I hadn't exactly expected Noelle to come, but it would have been a nice surprise. Still, I wasn't about to let their absence distract me. I had a mission to accomplish here, with or without them. Over the past hour, not only had Carolina and I managed to answer each and every one of Mr. Hathaway's objections, but we had already started to turn the crowd to our side. I credited Carolina's charm and my seemingly bottomless bank account for the change in tide.

Of course, now Hathaway had brought out the big guns. Speaking at the podium was Mr. Thatcher Phillips, a representative from the county development committee, who had come armed with a laundry list of complaints he had just finished reading aloud. He reminded me of the creepy guy who played Mr. Potter in *It's a Wonderful Life*, a movie I saw at least part of every Christmas season. He just had this air about him like his main goal in life was to suck any and all joy out of it.

"So you see, Miss Grant, Miss Brennan, all of these plans will need to be revised, which will surely mean weeks of additional work for your architect," he said haughtily, folding up his list and tucking it into the inside pocket of his tweed jacket. He pushed his bifocals up on his bulbous nose and folded his hands over his ample belly. "I'm afraid that means a delay to the start of the project of at least two months."

Behind the long table on the dais, Mr. Hathaway smiled into his hand. Is it wrong that I kind of wanted to smack him? What no one seemed to understand was that two months was not an option. In two *days* the entire Billings community was going to be descending on Easton, expecting to see some ribbon cutting. There was no way this weekend was going by without me wielding a giant pair of scissors.

"Actually, we have the revised plans right here," I said, pushing my chair back and standing. Mr. Hathaway sat up straight as Carolina handed me a hard blueprint carrier, which I brought up to the podium. "In both paper and digital format."

Mr. Phillips's waddle quivered and he appeared, for a moment, flummoxed. "Yes, well, we'll still need to review these and the process could take—"

"I'm willing to pay the admittedly exorbitant fee to rush the documents through," I said, smiling even though my heart was pounding nervously.

You're a Lange, I told myself. *You know you are. Make them believe it.*

"And since your very own staff architect oversaw the drawing up of these plans yesterday, I can't imagine there will be any objections to our starting the project this weekend, as scheduled, with his good-faith approval."

I turned and smiled at the county's architect, Jack Lagos, who sat just behind Carolina. He was handsome in an older, rugged kind of way, with his frayed jacket and chin scruff. Carolina had called him on Tuesday evening and he, like almost everyone else she met, had been unable to resist her enthusiasm. The two of them had worked with her design team all day on Wednesday, through the night, and most of today.

"Of . . . of course," Mr. Phillips said. "If you're willing to pay the fee and if Mr. Lagos approves . . ."

"I do, sir," Jack said, pushing himself halfway to standing. "You're not going to find any fault with those plans, I assure you."

"All . . . all right, then." Mr. Phillips cleared his throat. "Then I have nothing further."

As he turned back toward the dais, holding the blueprint roll, he looked at Mr. Hathaway and shrugged helplessly. I returned to our table as Carolina rose from her own chair. She surreptitiously gave me a very low high-five, then tugged on the lapels of her white linen jacket, which she wore over crisp jeans and a yellow T-shirt. It was amazing how she managed to look businesslike, casual, and pretty all at the same time.

"Esteemed members of the board, we have now competently answered each of your concerns, from the problem of privacy to the safety of the site to disruption of classes to the county's admirable green initiatives," she said firmly. "But if I might add one last point of interest?"

Mrs. Whittaker, my friend Walt Whittaker's grandmother, leaned forward in her seat, folding her gnarled fingers together atop the table. "Go ahead, Miss Grant."

Carolina paced out from behind our table, looking much like a chic lawyer from some procedural crime drama. "It's no secret to any of us in the Easton community that our school has had some . . . setbacks over the past two years."

There was much squirming and squeaking of chairs at this reference to our school's serious run of bad luck, but no one said a word.

"Time and again we've seen our good name splashed in the headlines and dragged through the mud," Carolina continued, pacing
before the board. "Some of the things that have been written and said
about this place are, unfortunately, true, but many of them are not.
This has unfairly tarnished our image in the private school community, not to mention the world at large."

At this point she turned dramatically to face the board. "I sub-
mit that the *Go Green!* experience will go a long way toward reversing
this negative publicity trend and putting Easton back on the map as a
progressive, forward-thinking, community-driven school where the
faculty and staff care not only about the students, but about the environment as well."

A few of the board members began to murmur with interest and
the crowd rippled with excited whispers.

"Just think about it," I put in, standing again. "Front-page photos,
not of crime scenes, but of students pitching in together to rebuild
something that was lost."

"Exactly!" Carolina said, snapping her fingers. My chest welled
with pride. "Headlines not about murder and mayhem, but about the
county's noble efforts to protect our environment, and Easton's particular role in leading the fight."

"We'll be supporting not only green businesses, but local businesses as well," I said, standing next to Carolina. "The opportunities
for positive publicity are endless, and will cost the school nothing."

"Not one cent." Carolina smiled.

"Honestly? I think we'd all be fools to let an opportunity like this one pass us by," I said boldly, looking Headmaster Hathaway in the eye.

Behind me, Vienna and London let out a whoop, and the left side of the room—the side where most of the students were sitting—erupted in applause. If my MT was among them, I hoped he or she could tell how grateful I was to them for helping me score this huge victory. Without the mystery texter, I never would have known that Carolina existed. I grinned out at the crowd, and it was all I could do to refrain from taking a bow.

"All right, all right," Headmaster Hathaway said, sitting forward and gesturing for quiet. "Enough with the propaganda, Miss Brennan."

I felt the sting of his insult, but let it go. It was his last-ditch effort to make me seem foolish, and it wasn't going to work. I could already tell by the smiles and the confident nods in my direction that we'd turned the board in our favor. Headmaster Hathaway was going down.

Mr. Hathaway took a deep breath and blew it out through his mouth, his chest deflating considerably.

"We will now put it to a vote," he said reluctantly. "All in favor of allowing Miss Brennan and the people at *Go Green!* to go ahead with the Billings reconstruction as scheduled, say 'aye.'"

There was a loud chorus of "ayes" from the board. The students cheered loudly. I think most of them were just psyched at the possibility of seeing their faces on TV, but that was enough for me. I suddenly couldn't stop grinning.

"Those opposed?" Mr. Hathaway asked pointlessly. He looked up and down the dais as silence reigned.

"The ayes have it," he said flatly. "Congratulations, Miss Brennan. I sincerely hope you know what you're doing."

The large hall erupted in applause. The headmaster stared me down from the front of the room as my friends gathered me in a group hug.

"Omigod, Reed! That was so awesome!" Amberly trilled.

Just as I stepped back, Paige, Missy, and Paige's twin, Daniel, stormed down the aisle. Daniel passed so close to me his jacket brushed my hand. I recoiled like I'd been burned, his violent temper tantrums down on St. Barths all but seared into my memory.

Paige and Missy barreled on, but he stopped, looking me up and down like I was vermin. "You're in way over your head, Podunk," he spat. Then he yanked his jacket closed and followed his twin outside, letting the door bang shut firmly behind him.

Twilight was just descending on the Easton campus as I sat down on one of the many stone benches dotting the quad. The air was warm and scented with honeysuckle. It was the kind of evening that made me want to take a deep breath and just be.

Unfortunately, my cell phone had other ideas.

"Hello? This is Reed Brennan," I said, answering the fifth call in as many minutes. As much as I wanted to cling to the high of our victory at the board meeting, the world wasn't about to let me. My many bags, papers, and poster rolls slipped out of my hands and tumbled to the ground at my feet. One of the posters bounced off and came to rest under a nearby birch tree. I sighed and just left it there.

"Miss Brennan? This is Lissa Knight." I racked my brain, trying to remember who, exactly, Lissa Knight was. One of the Billings alumnae, undoubtedly, but I'd just talked to four of them in a row and my brain was too fried to remember anything about this one. "I've heard there are some issues with the ribbon-cutting ceremony? I've already had my assistant charter a plane for myself and the other Dallas-area alumnae, and if I have to cancel it I need to know as soon as—"

"You don't have to cancel anything," I said, closing my eyes and praying for patience. "I've just come from a board hearing and I can guarantee you the ribbon-cutting ceremony *will* proceed as planned this Saturday morning, and all the other events are on as well."

"You're sure," she said. It was more of a statement than a question.

"I'm sure. I promise I wouldn't waste your valuable time if I wasn't one hundred percent positive we were going forward as scheduled," I assured her, trying for my most responsible voice.

As long as nothing else goes wrong in the next twenty-four hours, I thought, gritting my teeth.

"Well, all right, then." Her tone brightened considerably. "I'll let the others know."

"Would you?" I said gratefully, collapsing into the back of the bench and slumping down slightly. "That would be *so* helpful."

"Absolutely. I look forward to meeting you in person, Miss Brennan," Lissa said. "Good-bye."

"Me as well," I replied, then almost gagged. Was that even close to good grammar? "Good-bye."

I hung up the phone and groaned, dipping my head toward my knees. Someone sat down next to me, and I recognized by the polished, pointed toes of her shoes and signature musky scent that it was Noelle.

"Bad day?"

"Not entirely," I said, lifting my face and flipping my thick hair back. I sat up straight, feeling the need to keep up appearances with her as much as I did with all the alums. Lately, when I was around Noelle, all I wanted to do was prove to her that I was doing the right thing. "In fact, the board voted to let us go ahead as planned."

Noelle rested her arm on the back of the bench, gazing out across campus, taking in the beautiful pink and purple sky. The torchlights lining the walks suddenly flickered to life, painting a quaint and peaceful picture, the kind of warm, scenic shot Tiffany would have loved to have captured on her camera. The kind of image the Easton Academy catalog would have gladly slapped on its cover.

"I heard," she said, with a sour twist of her lips. "So why with the groaning and moaning?"

"I guess the rumors got ahead of me," I said, holding up the phone as the screen lit up once again. "All the alums and their assistants are calling to make sure everything's okay." I sighed and hit ignore. "I never realized that explaining and ass-kissing could be so exhausting."

Noelle looked me over. "You do look tired, Reed. And stress lines do *not* become you," she added, waving a finger around my brow area. I batted her hand away. "I'm just saying! Why don't you just let this whole Billings thing go? You're only here for one more year anyway. Why don't you try focusing on other things? Things that you can actually control?"

I blinked. What, exactly, made her think I couldn't control the Billings reconstruction? Hadn't I just proved beyond a shadow of a doubt that I could take on anything and anyone?

"Just live in Pemberly, spend your weekends at Cornell with lover-boy like you know you're going to anyway, graduate with honors, and put it all behind you," she added, leaning back.

"Is that what you're going to do? Just put it all behind you?"

Put me *behind you?* I added silently, feeling like a needy loser.

She pressed her lips together, giving me a condescending look that made my toes curl. "It's hard to explain, but there's something that changes when you get this close to the end," she said, gazing out at the quad again. Couples strolled hand in hand, enjoying the warm evening. A gaggle of freshman girls giggled their way across campus toward the solarium. Off in the distance, a church bell clanged. "You suddenly start to feel . . . no, you start to *know*, that none of this . . . it just doesn't matter, Reed."

Now my fingers curled into fists. Didn't she realize what she was saying? That this place that I loved despite everything, this place that had changed my life, didn't matter? That *I* didn't matter? That none of the crap we'd been through together over the past two years mattered?

I swallowed hard, not wanting to voice these thoughts. Not wanting to give her the opportunity to look down on me that way again. Like I was some pathetic middle schooler begging for her attention.

"I hate to say this, Noelle, but Billings . . . it's part of our heritage," I reminded her, shifting in my seat to face her. My phone rang again and I hit ignore as quickly as possible. "The Billings School for Girls was founded by our ancestors. I'm just trying to keep a part of that alive. Don't you care about that at all?"

Noelle lifted her shoulders, then let them fall. "That's all in the past. And after everything that's happened, I think we should keep it there. It has nothing to do with us."

I stared at her, wondering if she really believed that. Even when Josh walked up behind Noelle, hovering at the end of the bench, I didn't break eye contact.

"Hey, guys," he said tentatively. "What's up?"

Noelle sighed audibly and stood, lifting her bag onto her shoulder. "Maybe you can talk some sense into her, Hollis. I'm out of ideas. And quite honestly, I'm starting to be bored by this whole thing."

I let out a disbelieving bark of a laugh as she walked purposefully away. Josh slowly, tentatively sat down next to me and touched my shoulder, drawing a circle on my sweater with his thumb.

"What was that all about?" he asked.

"Just Noelle trying once again to squash all my hopes and dreams." The phone rang and I jammed my finger into the screen over the word "ignore." Then I turned it off and tossed it into my bag, already dreading the ten million calls I'd have to return later. I turned toward Josh. "She still wants me to give up on Billings, even though we just scored the board's approval. She thinks I should be focusing on 'other things,'" I told him, throwing in some highly sarcastic air quotes.

Josh tilted his head and chewed his lip, something he seemed to do often when he had something to say, but knew I wouldn't like it. I felt my heart drop. "Well, there *is* a lot of other stuff going on."

"Josh!" I wailed.

"Just hear me out," he said, putting his hand on my knee. "We have finals next week, then graduation, and we haven't even nailed down our plans for the summer yet. We've got all these parties and you've got the awards ceremony. . . . It's just a lot to pack in, that's all."

I turned my knees away from him in indignation. My insides felt crammed uncomfortably beneath my ribcage. Why couldn't I get just a teeny bit of support for something that mattered to me so much?

But even as I fumed, I couldn't help picturing the stack of assignments on my desk back in my room. And the dozens of unanswered e-mails and texts from my friends. Not to mention the fact that my calendar was so jammed I was running out of space to type in new events and appointments.

"And not that I want to be known for taking Noelle's side, but this whole thing seems like it depresses her every time it comes up," he said, looking off in the direction of Pemberly. "I almost feel . . . bad for her."

That got my attention. No one ever felt bad for Noelle Lange. Least of all Josh. And he was right, of course. Noelle had been through a horrible thing. Was Josh that much more in tune with my best friend's emotional state than I was?

Ugh. I loathed myself. Here I was, whining about how no one was supporting me, when all the while Noelle was needing *my* support.

I looked down at the mess of bulging bags and plans and papers and checklists and felt exhausted all over again, like I could just curl up in my bed and sleep for days. Maybe Noelle and Josh were both right. Maybe I'd taken on too much and lost sight of what was important in the process. Not just Noelle, but my other friends as well. This was supposed to be all about the Billings Girls, but other than at meals I'd barely seen any of them lately, and a lot of them would be graduating soon—Ivy, Tiffany, Rose, Portia, London, Vienna, Shelby. Wasn't I a total hypocrite if I ignored all of them in the name of Billings?

In the distance a construction vehicle roared to life. Carolina waved her arms in the air, directing the driver, and the last ray of sun glinted off the lens of Christopher's camera. It looked like someone was wasting no time in getting the project up and running again.

But that didn't mean I couldn't take a step back and take some time to deal with what was really important. Starting with my friendship with Noelle.

I narrowed my eyes and looked over at Josh. "I hate you, you know that?"

He smiled and put his arms around me. "Yes. But only when I'm right."

ALL ABOUT NOELLE DAY

The lunch crowd at the Driscoll Hotel restaurant on a Friday afternoon was not exactly hip and happening. Occupying the prime tables near the windows were a few middle-aged men in business suits, locked in quiet conversation as they pushed their steak frites around on their plates. In the center of the room, where everyone could see them and they wouldn't be tarnished by the sun's harmful rays, were a few tables full of little old ladies in pastel suits, their legs crossed at the ankles, their lipstick perfectly applied, and their hair sprayed to a shine. The maître d' led me and Noelle to a corner table, tucking us away from the rest of the clientele, and I surreptitiously slid my phone out of my Chloé bag and placed it atop my thigh under the linen tablecloth.

When I looked up, I caught a glimpse of auburn hair and saw Paige and Daniel Ryan just getting up from a table a few settings away. She shot me a scathing look and my palms began to sweat. I just couldn't get away from these people. I prayed they wouldn't come over to say hello to Noelle, and said a silent thank-you when they both turned and headed for the door.

"Taking the day off from classes to squire me to the Driscoll and a secluded corner table?" Noelle said, arching an eyebrow at me as she opened her menu. "I hope you're not planning to propose."

I laughed and scanned the specials menu, then placed the huge folder on my appetizer plate. "No, nothing like that," I said, lacing my fingers together atop the leatherbound menu. "I just . . . I've noticed you've been kind of down lately and I thought it'd be cool to take the afternoon off and hang out."

Noelle shook her head, an amused smile lighting her eyes. "I have *not* been down." She lifted her thick hair over her shoulders and reached for her water goblet. Somehow her strong arms already looked tan in her white sleeveless dress. At least, for once, she wasn't wearing black. "I don't *do* down."

In my lap, my phone vibrated. The text read:

IN LOBBY, CMING 2 U!

"Where in the world did you come up with *that* theory, Glass-Licker?"

I smirked, wondering how she'd react if I told her Josh was the one who had noticed it. "Whatever. The point is, I have a little surprise for you."

I turned and looked over my shoulder at the double oak doors, thrown open wide to the lobby.

"Oh, God. It's not a stripper, is it?" Noelle said, leaning sideways to see past me. She brought her fingertips to her temples. "Please tell me it's not some cheesy stripper."

"Oh, it's way better than that."

Just then Kiran Hayes and Taylor Bell walked into the room, spotted us, and let out a collective, but tastefully understated, squeal. Kiran grabbed Taylor's hand and they rushed over to us in their high heels, catching curious and lustful glances from the men at the window tables. Kiran, at almost six feet tall, cut a stunning figure in a skintight royal blue dress and black heels, her short, dark hair tucked behind her ears. Taylor's blond curls hung loose around her face, and her red cap-sleeve dress was belted by a black ribbon, accentuating her curves. Noelle's jaw dropped when she saw them, and she rose from her chair.

"Oh my God! I can't believe it!" Noelle gasped.

That was when I knew for sure she was surprised. Blurting without thinking was not Noelle's way. They all double-air-kissed, clutching hands and grinning as I got up to hug them hello.

"What're you guys doing here?" Noelle asked.

I held my breath, hoping neither of them would mention that they'd flown in for the Billings ribbon-cutting ceremony tomorrow, and that I'd added this lunch to their itineraries at the last minute. I'd rather Noelle believe it was the other way around.

"We're here for you, babe!" Kiran announced, giving Noelle a squeeze. Perfect answer.

"We have declared today All About Noelle Day!" Taylor added.

"Isn't that every day?" Noelle joked.

All of us laughed and I found myself staring at Noelle's smile. I hadn't seen it in weeks. Possibly months. Not a real one, anyway. As we all sat down around the table and the maître d' hurried over with two more menus, I couldn't stop grinning. It felt just like old times.

But then I heard it again. That odd snicker I'd heard in the hall at school the other day. I quickly turned in my seat and, sure enough, two tables over, a girl with blond hair, wearing a light blue plaid dress, sat alone, whispering into her cell. My pulse thrummed in my veins as I stared at the back of her head, just willing her to turn, willing her to finally show herself. Then she put the phone down and lifted a finger, summoning her waiter. As she turned I felt as if I was going to black out from the tension, the strain, the anticipation. But then I saw her long nose and brown eyes and realized it wasn't Ariana at all.

"Everything all right, Reed?" Taylor asked. "You look . . . sickly."

"Everything's fine," I said, turning toward the table again and forcing a smile. I looked around at the three of them and tried to shake the last inklings of fear. "In fact, it couldn't be better."

"Now *this* is what I'm talking about," Kiran said, leaning into the railing at the stern of Noelle's father's sailboat as it raced along the Connecticut coastline. I stood next to her and looked out at the view, which was rather spectacular. Huge mansions hovered over the water, interspersed with older, more modest Cape Cod houses. Seagulls cawed overhead, diving toward the water in pursuit of their prey. The only thing bluer than the sky was the water, and the sun glinted off its choppy surface, making everything glitter and gleam.

I tipped my face toward the sun and sighed, feeling completely relaxed. I had put Vienna and London in charge of dealing with any last-minute planning issues that might arise for this weekend's events, so my phone had remained relatively silent for the last couple of hours. Not having to hear that incessant beeping and ringing was like a mini-vacation.

"You know, I've been all over the world, but this is still one of my favorite spots," Kiran added, turning around and pushing her dark sunglasses up into her hair. "I don't know why I ever left."

I glanced over at Taylor, who sat on one of the cushioned benches at the rear of the boat, and Noelle, who was laid out on a blue-and-white striped Ralph Lauren towel in her shorts and sweater, her face tipped toward the sun. Each of us tensed just slightly, not so much that anyone outside our circle would have noticed, but we all sensed it and knew why. Kiran had a good reason for leaving. She, Noelle, and Taylor had all been expelled from Easton after Thomas Pearson was murdered. They, along with Ariana Osgood, had brought him out to the woods that night and left him there to fend for himself. Ariana had been the one to go back and kill him, so she had gone to some cushy millionaire's prison called the Brenda T. Trumball Correctional Facility for Women, while Noelle, Kiran, and Taylor had received probation, community service, and the aforementioned expulsions.

Of course, there was now the possibility that Ariana had somehow busted out and was stalking me all over campus.

I looked out across the stern, my heart pounding suddenly from all these Ariana-related thoughts. Part of me wanted to tell my friends about the strange, elusive blond-girl sightings I'd had over the past few days, but I bit down on my tongue. They'd just tell me I was crazy.

"So you've just spaced on the multimillion-dollar modeling contract?" Taylor joked, reaching for a flute of champagne. There was quite a spread on the low table at the center of the stern—champagne, strawberries and cream, a huge variety of chocolates—all the Billings Girls' favorite things.

"Oh yeah, that. For a second there I almost forgot what a huge, honking success story I am," Kiran joked. She dropped onto a cushion on the floor next to the table, folding her long, perfect legs under her, and plucked a strawberry from the bowl.

"Actually, I think we've all done pretty well, considering," Taylor said pragmatically. "I'm off to Oxford in the fall, Noelle will be ruling Yale, and Reed here has become a businesswoman and developer at the ridiculously advanced age of seventeen."

Kiran and I each lifted a glass. "Go us!" I said.

Noelle pushed herself up on her elbows. "I'll take one of those."

I handed her a glass and she sucked down half its contents.

"So tell me all about last night, Noelle. Was our little Glass-Licker as amazing as everyone's saying?" Kiran asked, leaning forward.

My stomach and heart switched places as I waited for Noelle's reaction.

"Actually, I wouldn't know," Noelle said, looking out across the ocean. "I couldn't make it."

"Are you kidding?" Taylor asked. She slid off the bench and onto the floor, pulling her bag onto her lap. "Oh my God, then you have to see it."

"What do you mean, see it?" I asked.

Taylor extricated her laptop, popped it open, and toggled to YouTube. "Someone posted it last night," she said, her fingers flying over the keys. "Here. Check it out."

She turned the screen around, adjusted the contrast to fight the sun glare, and there I was, standing alongside Carolina, making my case. Noelle sat up and Kiran scooted around the table to hover over our shoulders. When I saw how self-righteous I looked, giving my little speech, I hid my face behind my hands. My voice sounded nasal through the speakers and I just wanted to cringe.

"Honestly? I think we'd all be fools to let an opportunity like this one pass us by," I heard myself say.

"Nice!" Kiran cheered, kneading my shoulders. "Damn, girl. Very diva."

The video ended and I peeked through my fingers. Noelle smirked and took a swig of champagne. "Wow. And you say you're not a Lange." She looked me up and down quickly. "Daddy would have been very proud."

My hands dropped and I found myself beaming. I knew it must have taken a huge effort for her to say that, and I appreciated it more than I could have ever expressed. Noelle gazed at me for a moment, then stood and walked to the back of the boat. Taylor slapped her laptop closed and the rest of us joined Noelle. My heart felt heavy and excited at the same time. Noelle had one hand curled around the railing and I placed my fingers right next to hers, taking a deep breath.

"Noelle . . . I'm sorry if it seems like I've been ignoring your feelings about all this," I said, as Kiran stepped up next to me and Taylor leaned in next to Noelle. "So if you're really and truly against this whole thing, I'll drop it. I'll call Carolina right now and put the kibosh on. I swear."

"Wait. You're against Billings making a comeback?" Kiran blurted. "Are you sure you're Noelle Lange?"

Noelle ignored her. "Really?" she said, pulling her ponytail over her right shoulder as she turned to look at me. "You'd do that?"

I swallowed hard. "Yeah. I would. You're more important to me than Billings."

There was a long, loaded moment of silence. Taylor and Kiran exchanged a nervous look. Water slapped against the sides of the boat and the sound of a yacht's horn carried over the ocean.

"Okay, fine," Noelle said finally, rolling her eyes. "You and Billings have my blessing."

"Are you serious?" I exclaimed.

"How could I stand in the way of your budding career as a real estate tycoon?" she joked, taking a sip of her champagne.

I threw my arms around her. "Thank you, thank you, thank you! Noelle, you have no idea what this means to me."

"Oh, I think I do," she replied, giving me a quick squeeze.

"Well, I say we celebrate!" Kiran announced.

"I'm so confused as to what we've been doing up till now. . . ." Taylor teased her, narrowing her eyes.

"Ha-ha. More champagne!" Kiran cried, grabbing the bottle from the silver ice bucket.

She refilled all our glasses and we clinked them together once again. "To the new Billings," I said.

"To the new Billings," they echoed.

We sipped our champagne, the afternoon sunlight glinting off our flutes, and I smiled, trying to lock this moment in my mind. Who knew how many chances the four of us would have to be together over the next few years, what with Taylor in the UK and Kiran bopping all over the world?

"So, how long are you guys sticking around?" Noelle asked, grabbing a chocolate from the tray.

"Oh, I'm here through graduation," Kiran said, waving a hand. "I cancelled all my appearances so I could hang with you girls."

"Me too," Taylor said. "I pretty much completed the credits for graduation in December. And I'm dying to go to the Easton graduation party."

"Do you think it's as crazy as they say it is?" I asked.

For the last few weeks I'd been hearing rumors about this graduation bash. Rumors that made a rural Pennsylvanian like me blush.

"Crazier," Noelle said gleefully. "I can't wait!"

As the three of them started to share stories they'd heard about graduation parties past—tales of mass skinny dipping, near ODs, and random hookups—my phone beeped. I tugged it out of my bag and checked the screen. I had one new text. From an unknown number.

It was MT. I glanced around at my friends to make sure they weren't watching me, then opened the text. My heart all but stopped when I saw the short message.

U SHLD FIGURE OUT A WAY 2 LOCK UR DOOR.

My knees gave out beneath me. Luckily I was close enough to the bench to fall down on the cushions and make it look like the tipping of the boat had thrown me off balance. My fingers shook as I placed my champagne glass carefully on the table.

"You okay, Glass-Licker?" Noelle asked.

"She never could hold her alcohol," Kiran joked.

"I'm fine. I just need to make a quick call," I told them.

"Aw! Hollis is that clingy, huh?" Noelle joked.

Kiran and Taylor made kissing noises, cracking themselves up until they saw they weren't going to get a rise out of me. I was too busy speed-dialing Ivy. She picked up on the second ring.

"Hey, Reed. What's up?"

"Are you at Pemberly?" I asked under my breath.

"Yeah. Why?"

"Can you go over to my room and check on it?"

"Check on it?" she said, confused. Even so, I could hear her bed-springs creak and her door open. "What do you mean?"

I clenched my eyes closed, trying to be patient. "Just make sure nothing's out of place or anything."

I heard the telltale sound of my door hinges squealing and held my breath. In my mind's eye I saw my laptop cracked on the floor, all my clothes whipped into twisted piles, posters and photos ripped and smashed. I waited for a stunned gasp, a whispered expletive, but there was nothing.

"Everything looks fine," she said. "Reed, what's going on?"

"Nothing." I let out a relieved sigh. "I just got another text from MT," I whispered, glancing over my shoulder at the others. "Maybe he was just messing with me."

"Well, it's all good," she said. "In fact, I never noticed this before, but you are obsessively neat."

"Okay, we'll talk about my mild OCD later," I promised her. "Do me a favor and just . . . I don't know . . . keep an ear out. If you hear anyone in there, call security."

"I'm on it," Ivy replied.

"Thanks, Ivy. I gotta go."

I hung up the phone and rejoined my friends. Kiran turned up the volume on the iPod dock and started to sing along to the music, twirling Taylor under her arm as Noelle swayed to the music, grabbing herself a strawberry. I did my best to get in on the fun, but inside I couldn't seem to unclench.

And I knew I wouldn't be able to until I saw my room for myself.

NOT QUITE RIGHT

The four of us spent half the afternoon talking about the plans for the new Billings, and I forced myself to relax, but the second we zoomed through the Easton gates, the tension returned. By the time Noelle swung her Jaguar convertible into a parking space right in front of Pemberly and hit the brakes, I was filled with dread.

"You okay?" Noelle asked, noticing my sudden pallor.

"Yeah." I unhooked my seatbelt and attempted a smile. "Just remembered I have a ton of work to do."

"Well, hop to it, Junior," Noelle said, patting me on top of my head. She twirled her keys around one finger and got out of the car. "I, graduating senior that I am, am going to ignore my work and head over to Coffee Carma for a latte."

I rolled my eyes at her.

Noelle closed her door, then leaned against it, over the open expanse of the convertible. "Seriously, though, Reed. Thanks for today. I had fun."

I smiled for real this time. "Me too."

She headed around the dorm for the quad and I ran for the front door. Noelle may have been trying to rub my nose in her freedom, but I was kind of glad she was going elsewhere. It meant I could sprint inside and take the stairs instead of the elevator and be at my room in half the time.

I threw open the door to my room and stood frozen on the threshold, looking around. At first I felt a slight twinge of relief. Ivy was right. Nothing looked out of place. But as I stepped inside I realized that wasn't entirely the case. Nothing was out of place, but something was missing. Namely, the Billings blueprints.

Leaving the door open, I lunged to the corner where I'd left the poster roll containing all Carolina's blueprints for the new design. It was gone. I hit my knees to check under the bed, but there was nothing there aside from the usual under-the-bed storage and a stray pair of shoes. Cursing under my breath, I shoved open my closet and ransacked the floor, just in case I'd tossed them in there and forgotten about it. Which I knew I hadn't.

There was nothing. The blueprints were gone. I shoved my hands into my hair as I turned around and my eyes fell on my computer. Had I left my laptop open like that?

"Sonofa—"

I leaned over my desk and booted up my computer. The Billings Construction folder was gone from the desktop. I checked the trash. Wiped out. I hadn't had time to back up the files before I went out this morning, which meant they were just gone. Carolina had some of the information, obviously, and I had everyone's numbers and e-mails stored in my phone, but all my notes were in that folder. All my ideas and whims and reminders. All of it had been deleted.

"No," I said under my breath, lowering myself onto the edge of my bed. "No, no, no."

I drew my knees up under my chin and clung to my shins. Suddenly all the old horrifying feelings came rushing back over me. All the dread and fear and sense of violation I'd felt back when Sabine stalked me last semester. That feeling that nothing was sacred, that nothing was safe, that nothing was mine. Someone had been in my room. Someone had rifled through my things. Someone had walked around this very space—my space—like they were entitled to it.

My heart clenched over and over and over until it felt like it couldn't take it anymore. What else had they done? What else had they taken? What else had they tarnished?

And how had MT known they were here?

Someone passed by the open door of my room and I nearly jumped out of my skin. But it was only Josh. He did a double take, like he was surprised to find me here. My hands clutched the bedspread at my sides as I waited for my pulse to come back from its sprint.

Josh paused and looked down the hall, in the direction from which he'd come. My eyes narrowed automatically as he braced both hands against either side of the doorway and leaned his whole body forward into the room.

"Um, hey," he said.

Um, hey?

"Hi." I uncurled my legs and placed my feet carefully on the floor. Part of me didn't want him to notice my terrified body language—didn't want him to worry—but part of me was also wondering . . . how could he *not* notice it? Why hadn't he immediately asked me what was wrong?

Finally he stepped into the room. "What's up?" he asked, shoving his hands into the pockets of his jeans and looking around the room. Looking everywhere but at me.

My heart gave an extra-hard thump. He was acting really weird. He didn't . . . he couldn't . . . there was no way he had something to do with the missing stuff, was there? He wouldn't try to sabotage Billings. Not when he knew how much it meant to me. Not when he knew how Sabine had tortured me last fall by infiltrating my room. But then why was he so blatantly keeping his distance from me?

"Nothing," I said flatly.

"So did you have fun with Noelle and them?" he asked, looking me in the eye for the first time.

"Yeah. It was great," I said. I tried to infuse my words with enthusiasm. "She was so excited when she saw Kiran and Taylor. It was awesome."

Josh smiled and suddenly, just like that, he was Josh again. He sat down next to me and knocked my shoulder with his. "Told ya so."

My heart relaxed slightly. "Didn't anyone ever tell you that everyone hates a guy who says 'I told you so'?"

"Oh, right." He reached for my hand and held it. "I think I *have* heard that somewhere."

I looked down at our fingers, at the sparkling aquamarine promise ring Josh had given me for my birthday, and suddenly felt like a colossal jerk for suspecting him. Josh may have hated Billings in the past, but he would never do anything to hurt me. Someone else had to be behind all this.

Which, of course, made me feel gross and violated and paranoid all over again. I opened my mouth to tell Josh about MT and the thefts, but my throat closed over the words. I didn't want to stress him out and make him worry. And maybe just the teeniest, tiniest bit of me didn't want to see how he'd react, just in case he wasn't surprised.

I was going to tell him eventually. I would. I just had to sort out a few things first for myself.

"I'm glad it all worked out," Josh said, giving my hand a squeeze.

"Yeah," I said distractedly, my eyes scanning the room for more items out of place, trying to discern if anything else might be missing. "Yeah, me too."

CUTTING THE RIBBON

"And now I'd like to introduce the driving force behind this entire project," Carolina said into the microphone, leaning toward the podium. "Miss Reed Brennan."

She threw out her arm in my direction and I stood up shakily from my chair on the stage. The crowd clapped and cheered and I gave them the widest smile I could manage, considering how nervous I was. The sun was blinding, but I could still make out the surprisingly large crowd gathered at the base of the five-foot-high stage. Not only were there dozens of older Billings alumnae represented, but some of my more recently graduated friends were there too. Natasha Crenshaw, my former roommate, stood at the front of the pack with Walt Whittaker and Dash McCafferty, who held hands with Noelle in the sun. Josh stood next to Noelle, along with Ivy and Tiffany, whose camera was at the ready. Several reporters, some with microphones and cameras, others with tape recorders or notepads, were focused on me. Behind me on the stage, all the members of the Billings Board of Directors were seated in their chairs, waiting to hear my speech. I glanced down at Headmaster Hathaway as I passed him by and was almost surprised he didn't shoot out a leg to trip me.

"Thank you, everyone, for that amazing welcome, and thanks for simply being here. Before I get started I'd like to thank Headmaster Hathaway and the Board of Directors for granting me the distinct honor of rebuilding Billings House." I looked over at the board, each member more distinguished-looking and proud than the last. "I wouldn't be here without your support."

Taking a deep breath, I faced the crowd. I had prepared a short speech, which I had practiced for anyone who would listen, and I had thought I was ready for this, but at that moment my head felt somehow heavy and light all at once. A slight breeze tickled the back of my neck and sent a foreboding skitter down my spine. I glanced over my shoulder quickly, feeling as if someone was watching me from behind. Across the yawning hole of the foundation, Larry Genovese stood with a dozen other workers, all clad in safety vests and hard hats, ready for their cue. As I scanned their faces, I saw a shock of blond hair as someone in a dark jacket ducked behind one of the trailers. My breath caught, but the creeper didn't appear again, and I was left wondering if I'd imagined it.

"Reed," Carolina said through her teeth. "Are you okay?"

I took another breath and nodded. *Don't let whoever broke into your room get you all paranoid. Don't let them ruin this moment,* I told myself as I faced forward again. *Don't let them have the power.*

"As many of you know, my background is different from most of the student population of Easton," I began. "I came here last year as a scholarship student, unsure of where I'd fit in, clueless as to what it meant to attend a private school. I remember staring out my window that first night, feeling so homesick it scared me. A huge part of me wanted to flee. I wanted to go back to Pennsylvania and the world I knew. And I might have done that, if it wasn't for the friends I found at Billings."

I looked down at Noelle and she gave me a closed-lipped, encouraging smile.

"That's not to say we didn't have our bumps at first, as we tried to get to know each other, as I began to understand their world, but before long I came to think of Billings as my true home, my housemates as my sisters. I began to realize what an honor it is to be a part of a grand tradition like Billings, and I was heartbroken when that tradition was taken away."

I paused for a moment as cameras clicked and a few people in the crowd murmured. Suddenly I recalled with perfect clarity how it felt that day when Noelle and I had come back to campus to find Billings flattened. The confusion, the devastation, the hopelessness. It was all I could do to keep from glancing over at Headmaster Hathaway accusatorily.

"But now I have a second chance. We all have a second chance. To make Billings what it should be. To make it what we all know it can be. A place where young women can live and work together, share ideas, share their dreams and goals, and foster a sense of support as they make their way out into the world."

Someone shouted and there was another round of applause from the alumnae dotted throughout the crowd.

"So now, it gives me great pleasure to invite Billings alum Carolina Grant and Headmaster Hathaway to help me cut the ribbon and officially get this project under way."

The various members of the press clamored for a better angle as Carolina, Mr. Hathaway, and I walked over to the shiny red ribbon tied between two orange cones at the top of the construction site. Mr. Hathaway's assistant handed us a huge pair of scissors, which Carolina and I both held onto. Then Mr. Hathaway pulled the ribbon taut for us so we could cut it. I looked up to smile for the cameras before doing the deed, and my eyes fell on Sawyer and Graham, who were standing right next to a klatch of Billings Girls, including Constance, Kiki, Astrid, Lorna, and Amberly. Sawyer had a grim smile on his face, but Graham looked like he was considering tackling me right into the gaping foundation hole behind me.

I gulped.

"Let's do this," Carolina whispered.

The slice of the scissors sounded like a steak knife being dragged across a sharpener. And then it was over and cheers filled the air. When I looked up again, both Sawyer and Graham were gone.

Mr. Hathaway shook my hand. On the far side of the foundation, a cement truck backed up, its barrel tipping toward the hole to release the wet cement for the basement. A crowd of well-wishers gathered around me, clasping my fingers, giving me hugs and air-kisses, posing for photos.

"Miss Brennan! Miss Brennan! If I could get a quick quote—"

"I was promised an interview—"

"If we could get all three of you over here for a picture—"

Everything was a blur of faces and microphones and smiles and kisses. And then, suddenly, a loud, crunching, creaking wail filled the air. Someone screamed. There were startled and panicked shouts, and before I knew what was happening, everyone around me was shoving me toward the edge of the deep hole.

"Omigod." Carolina gasped next to me. "No!"

And then, the crash. I stood on my toes to see what was going on, just in time to watch the cement truck fall backward into the foundation. The huge vehicle flipped over onto its back, landing on its still twisting barrel with a sickening and seemingly never-ending crunch of metal. On the far side of the foundation, workers scrambled down ladders, trying to get to the driver. It all happened so fast, yet I saw every last moment of it in crystal-clear slow motion. Horrifying slow motion.

"Get him out of there!" Headmaster Hathaway shouted.

Carolina screamed as the door of the cab opened and the driver dangled from the opening. If he fell the wrong way he'd be sucked under the turning cement barrel and crushed. Some brave workers edged close to the vehicle and stood under the open door. An odd, strangled screech escaped from my throat as the dangling man fell into their arms and was quickly dragged away. A few people started to applaud, but all I wanted to do was collapse. The cement truck continued to churn, gurgling fresh cement in massive globs all over the basement, its gears grinding as it dug a hole for itself in the dirt.

"Miss Brennan! Miss Brennan! What do you have to say about this accident?"

I turned around and at least ten microphones and recorders were shoved in my face. Whoever wasn't on me was on Carolina, and with each passing moment of our stunned silence the shouted questions grew more absurd.

"Did you have the proper permits?"

"Is that man certified to work with that kind of machinery?"

"How do you feel about endangering the lives of your fellow students?"

"What do you say to rumors that this site is cursed?"

Headmaster Hathaway's strong hand came down on my shoulder.

"Don't say a word," he hissed in my ear. "We have no comment at this time!" he shouted loudly.

Then he took my arm and dragged me out of there as fast as possible, barreling over whoever he needed to flatten on the way. I was grateful to him for sparing me, but even so, I knew he had another agenda in mind too—to keep me from blurting anything too tarnishing to the press. Apparently it would be a little while before Easton started to benefit from all that positive publicity I'd promised him.

CRAZY

"What did your crew chief say about the accident?" Ivy asked, pushing her dark hair over her shoulder as she leaned forward over the wide library table that afternoon. "How long is it going to set you back?"

We were trying to squeeze in some studying before tonight's cocktail party at Mitchell Hall, where I was sure to be answering tons of similar questions. The very idea made me feel exhausted.

"Yeah. How serious was it?" Kiki asked, popping a green Tic Tac into her mouth.

"They're going to work all night to try to clean up the mess and keep things on track," I said, trying not to let my stress come through. "Workers are already bailing out excess cement and smoothing out what they can, and they're bringing in some kind of huge crane to remove the truck."

"Thank God the driver wasn't hurt," Constance whispered, biting her lip. "That was so scary."

"I know," I replied, the heavy rocks in my gut rearranging themselves hastily. If someone had been seriously hurt today, I'd never be able to forgive myself.

"So how did it happen?" Tiffany asked. She'd been scrolling through her photos on her camera, but placed it down in the center of the table now. "Did something go wrong with the truck?"

"That's the thing," I said, my throat dry. "Both Larry and the driver said they checked everything out half an hour before the pouring. The truck was practically brand new and everything was in working order."

Ivy eyed me in a discerning way, then sat back in her chair. "You're not thinking what I think you're thinking, are you?"

"Aren't we all?" Astrid asked from the far end of the table, her dark eyes serious.

"What?" Constance asked blankly. "What are we all thinking?"

"That this wasn't an accident," Astrid, Ivy, and I said in unison.

"Oh, come on," Constance said. She dropped her forehead down onto her folded arms and whimpered. "Someone *else* is out to get us?"

"No, not us. Just the building," I assured her, though I wasn't completely certain. "Someone doesn't want Billings to be rebuilt. Today's 'accident' could have been their way of telling us to stop."

"Normally I'd say you're being paranoid, but around here . . ." Ivy trailed off and raised her eyebrows.

"Who?" Constance asked, raising her face only slightly, so that her nose rested on her hand and her mouth was still hidden. "Who would do this?"

"Yes, can you please just tell us who so we can have Portia sic the Armenian mafia on their asses?" Tiffany joked.

Everyone laughed uncomfortably. *Missy and Paige,* I wanted to say. But I knew they'd balk. Tiffany had been friendly with Paige back when she'd been a student here, and some of the other girls would still be friends with Missy if she'd let them. With no real proof, I didn't want to call them out. At least not yet.

"I would if I could, but I have no idea," I semi-lied.

A loud slam sounded on the other side of the library, and a couple of chairs scraped against marble.

"Get out of my face!" a familiar voice shouted.

"Was that Josh?" Ivy asked me, her dark eyes wide.

I jumped out of my chair as everyone else in the library turned to look. Josh was in the far corner at his favorite study carrel and Graham was standing next to him, his fists clenched. Josh turned and stormed away from Graham, striding right past our table with his canvas messenger bag bouncing against his hip. I opened my mouth to say something, but he was so focused and furious he didn't even see me. He got to the front door and shoved it open with the heel of his hand, disappearing out into the dark.

"What. The hell. Was that?" Kiki asked.

And then everyone in our immediate vicinity looked at me. I watched, my pulse thrumming in my ears, as Graham disappeared up the stairs to the English literature section.

"I don't know," I said, dropping my pencil on the table. "But I'm going to find out."

I hurried away from our table, half speed-walking, half jogging for the stairs. As I neared the middle step, I got the eerie, spine-tingling feeling that someone was watching me and I slowed my pace, glancing quickly over my shoulder. At least ten people looked away. Who was I kidding? Everyone was watching me this time.

By the time I got to the top of the stairs, I was out of breath, both from exertion and nerves. What was I doing following a guy who had done nothing but glare at me and piss off my boyfriend for the past few weeks? But I couldn't take it anymore. Down in St. Barths when we had first met, I had really liked Graham. He'd been so down-to-earth and funny and friendly. And I'd thought he'd liked me too. What had made him change so drastically in just a few short months?

I heard some books being slammed around somewhere to my right, and started searching. I found Graham in the third row and crossed my arms over my chest. He saw me from the corner of his eye and scoffed.

"What?" he blurted.

"Like you don't know," I whispered, walking toward him. "Graham, what the hell is going on with you lately?"

"Nothing," he said, shaking his head. He pushed over a book at the end of a shelf, dominoing all the others over in the process. Lifting his shoulders, he turned his palms toward me and moved to the next section. "I just can't stand that guy."

"Josh," I said. "You can't stand Josh."

"Bingo!" he said, his eyes lighting up with sarcasm.

"Graham, this makes no sense," I said, leaning back against the shelf as he shoved some hardcover books back and forth into one another. "You guys used to be friends."

"He doesn't understand the concept," he snapped.

"I know he had a history with your sister—"

Graham snorted and turned away from me, crossing to the other side of the aisle.

"But what are you going to do? Walk around being pissed at every guy she ever dated? Everyone who upset her in her life?" I asked.

One of the librarians walked past slowly, shooting us a silencing glare. Graham stopped messing with the books and finally turned to face me.

"You just don't get it, do you?" he said, shoving his hands under his arms, bunching up his striped cotton sweater in the process. "That guy is not stable, Reed."

My face burned, offended. "I know he's manic-depressive," I informed him. "That's old news. And as long as he takes his meds, he's fine."

"Yeah. You keep telling yourself that," Graham said sarcastically. He reached out and picked at a sticker on one of the shelves, an old label reading BRA–BRE.

My heart slammed against my rib cage and all of a sudden I was back in Mitchell Hall on the night Josh had been arrested on suspicion of Thomas's murder. He'd been so scared, so manic, so not himself. He'd gone off his medication without consulting his doctor, and he'd been acting odd for such a long time I had even started to suspect him myself. Was this why he'd been acting all shifty and forgetful lately? Had he gone off his meds again?

Graham watched me closely, almost like he could tell what I was thinking. I lifted my chin in defiance.

"I don't have to listen to this," I told him. "I know Josh. I know he's a good person."

"Oh my God, Reed! Can you just think about it for five seconds?" he blurted, stepping closer to me. "His roommate at our old school killed himself. Then my sister, his girlfriend, killed herself. Do you really think that's a coincidence?"

"Yes," I said firmly. "I do."

Graham shook his head slightly, looking me in the eye as if he felt sorry for me. "I like you, Reed. I really do. And my brother . . . he's, like, beyond in love with you."

I felt a warm and prickly sensation around my heart and averted my eyes. I knew how Sawyer felt about me, but that didn't mean I was comfortable with his brother saying it aloud.

"And it just makes me *sick* that you would choose a liar and a psycho like Josh Hollis over a good, honest guy like Sawyer."

My jaw dropped.

"Is that what this is all about?" I demanded. "Are you trying to play matchmaker here? Because you've picked a sick and twisted way to do it."

Graham blinked, then backed away. It was almost as if my words had just woken him up from some kind of crazy dream.

"No," he said, knocking his fists together as he stepped backward. "No. It's just . . . we just don't want you to end up like our sister, that's all. I'd hate to see that happen to you, Reed. I really would."

I swallowed hard, my heart lodged somewhere between my breast-plate and my voice box. Why did that sound more like a threat than an expression of concern? And what the hell did he mean by calling Josh a liar, anyway? I knew about Josh's medical history, his meds, his therapy.

"Just think about it, okay?" Graham implored as he reached the end of the stacks. "That's all I ask."

And with one last, pitying look, he was gone.

LIMB FROM LIMB

"That accident was just horrifying, Reed. Just horrifying," Janice Winthrop said, gesturing around with her mimosa. "I just hope you can find some way to reverse this bad PR, because otherwise . . ."

She let her thoughts trail off, raising her penciled-in eyebrows as she sipped her drink. I glanced around the crowded party room at Isabella's, the pretty restaurant I'd commissioned for the Billings Sunday brunch, just hoping that someone, anyone, would save me from this awful conversation.

"Well, I've been assured by my team that everything is already back on track," I told her, forcing a confident smile. "Personally, I think that when a project can bounce right back after an accident like that, it can only create *good* PR."

Janice frowned thoughtfully as she eyed me up and down. "I have to admire your pluck." Then she patted me on the arm with an icy hand. "Good luck, my dear. And do let me know if there's anything I can do," she said, then walked over to join a group of old friends near the buffet.

All around the sunlit room, Billings alums chatted with Easton faculty and students as they noshed on croissants and fruit. My friends circulated the room in small groups, talking up the former Billings Girls, punctuating their conversations with charming smiles and polite laughter. Everyone was doing their job, but all I wanted to do was go home and crawl back into bed. Left alone for the first time all morning, I decided to take advantage of the temporary freedom and made a beeline for the bathroom for a breather.

But once inside the gleaming, porcelain bathroom, I found myself staring into the mirror. Who was I kidding? A moment alone just meant a moment to obsess. All I could think about last night and this morning was Graham's rant. Specifically the part where he'd called Josh a liar. What did he mean by that? Did he mean that Josh knew something more about his roommate's and Jen Hathaway's deaths? Or did it mean that he'd gone off his meds and not told me?

Or maybe . . . maybe Josh *was* the one sabotaging the Billings project. Maybe Graham had somehow found out about it and was trying to warn me. But then why not just come out and say it? Besides, I just couldn't picture it. I couldn't picture Josh going behind my back. And I definitely couldn't picture him jeopardizing that worker's life yesterday. Unless he *had* gone off his meds and was having a seriously bad reaction—an uncontrollable reaction. Which would mean he was lying to me about *two* huge things.

I groaned and gripped the sides of the white pedestal sink. Why was all of this happening? Why now? I had way too much to do to be sitting here obsessing about crap like this.

I wondered if anyone back at Croton High ever had to deal with stalkers and murderers and mystery texters. My guess was no.

A knock at the door interrupted my thoughts. I quickly washed my hands and walked out, holding the door open for the woman who'd been waiting. I took a deep breath, steeling myself for more butt-kissing and explaining-away-of-disaster, and turned toward the restaurant.

"Um, Reed?"

I whirled around, startled. Sawyer hovered near the end of the short hallway, in front of a brocade bench, looking tense and uncomfortable. His blond hair hung over one eye and he wore a gray sport jacket over a wrinkled black T-shirt. I hugged my arms against the air-conditioned chill in the hall and tried to smile, wondering what he was doing here. I couldn't imagine that his father would have encouraged his attendance, even though the headmaster had been forced to show up for appearance's sake.

"Hey, Sawyer."

"You okay?" he asked.

"Yeah." I tried for a casual shrug. "Just kind of can't wait until this whole weekend is over. But then I guess I get to go back to stressing about finals, so . . ."

Sawyer cracked an understanding smile and pushed his hands deep into the pockets of his jeans. "Like the rest of us."

I nodded, wondering if he'd been waiting for me to come out of the bathroom, or if this meeting was just a coincidence. Sawyer toyed with a button on his jacket, twisting it around and around.

"Are *you* okay?" I asked.

He looked into my eyes, seeming to steel himself. Then he blew out a sigh, his cheeks puffing up and deflating.

"I heard about what happened with you and Graham," he said, biting his lip.

"Oh," I said, my heart fluttering with sudden nerves. "That."

"Yeah." He sat down on the bench behind him and pressed his hands together between his knees. "That."

The toilet inside the bathroom flushed. I moved over to the bench and sat next to Sawyer as the woman emerged and headed back to the party.

"I'm really sorry, Reed. Graham . . . he tries to be a good brother, but . . . he has no idea what he's talking about," Sawyer said, looking at up at me through that lock of blond hair.

"He seemed pretty adamant," I said.

"You have to understand, he and Jen, they were inseparable," Sawyer told me, sitting up straight. "I don't know if it was the twin thing or what, but they were best friends. When she died, it was like he died with her. He's had his good moments, don't get me wrong, but he's a different person than he used to be. And it's like he's always looking for someone to blame for it."

I shook my head. I couldn't imagine what it had been like for Graham, not to mention Sawyer. If my brother Scott ever died . . . I wasn't sure how I would ever get through it.

"Like Josh," I said.

"Yeah. Like Josh," he repeated, his blue eyes sad. He licked his lips and looked down at his lap. "And about the other stuff . . . the stuff about me and you—"

"It's okay," I said, my gut twisting in knots. "You don't have to say anything."

"No," he blurted, so vehemently it startled me. He wiped his palms on his jeans. "No, I do. I mean, I don't know what he said *exactly*, but there is something I want you to know."

My breath caught in my throat. *Please don't let him profess his undying love. Please, please, please.* That was something I definitely wouldn't be able to deal with on top of everything else. Sawyer reached over and took my hand. He tugged it toward him, holding it between our two knees. My first instinct was to draw it back, but it seemed so unnecessarily cruel. So I just sort of froze. Froze and prayed for this to be over quickly.

"All I want is for you to be happy," he said seriously, looking me in the eye. "That's really all I want. You know that, right? Even if it's with some other guy."

My heart thumped. Hard. Definitely not what I expected. And I had no idea how to respond.

"Okay," I said finally, awkwardly.

And then Josh walked into the hallway. Sawyer sprang to his feet, which of course just made the whole thing look even worse than it really was.

"Josh!" I said, standing. "Hey!"

There was something in his eyes as he looked at me right then, something I'd never seen before and knew right away I never wanted to see again. He looked like he wanted to tear me limb from limb. In that moment I couldn't breathe. I couldn't even think. And then, just as suddenly, it was gone.

"I should get back to my dad," Sawyer said.

He waited for Josh to move so that he could get past, but Josh stood his ground, forcing Sawyer to turn sideways so he could slide by. He lifted his hand in my direction before disappearing around the corner.

Josh's lower jaw shifted to the side, then righted itself. "Moving on already?" he said archly. "I haven't even graduated yet."

My pulse was still pounding from his awful glare. I just looked at him, trying to see the guy I loved and not the one who had just momentarily scared the crap out of me.

"I'm just kidding!" he said, cracking a grin. "Wow. Are you okay?"

He reached for my hands and I let him take them, but kept my distance otherwise, leaning back against the wall. His fingers were cold and calloused.

"I'm fine." I looked into his eyes, but there was nothing there other than jovial Josh. "You know I'm not interested in Sawyer."

"Of course I do." He moved his hands up my arms, enveloped me in a hug, and gave me a quick, dry kiss on the lips. "I was just messing around."

Then he let me go and turned toward the end of the hall. "So, you ready to get back in there? People are asking for you."

I took a deep breath and tried to calm the beating of my heart.

"Ready," I said, hazarding a smile.

He reached for my hand and then, just like that, we rejoined the party as if nothing was wrong. As if I wasn't starting to wonder, just the teeniest, tiniest bit, if Graham was onto something.

DISTRACTION

Josh was off his meds. It was the only reasonable explanation for all the odd behavior. As I sat in the solarium on Monday night along with Constance, Astrid, and Lorna, I couldn't stop staring at him. He was sitting on the other side of the room, alone, slumped in a chair with one hand against his temple. His focus was on a novel for English class, but beneath the table, one leg bounced up and down, like he was some kind of speed freak coming down from a high.

"So who do you guys think is going to win the scholar-athlete award for the seniors, Trey or Lance?" Astrid asked, taking a slug of her double espresso. "Because Trey's, like, freaking out about it."

"Oh, please. Trey has it in the bag," Lorna said. "He plays three varsity sports and was MVP in basketball. Lance is only on crew and fencing."

"Yeah, but Lance has the better grades," Constance pointed out. "And it *is scholar*-athlete."

"Exactly what Trey keeps saying," Astrid put in. "What do you think, Reed?"

"No contest," I said distractedly. "Trey'll win."

A pair of guys from the soccer team walked in through the side door and Josh nearly jumped out of his skin. A moment later Marc Alberro strolled close to Josh's table and Josh's head jumped up, as if he were startled. As if he was waiting for someone to attack him.

"Well, I know I'm not winning anything, but I don't care," Lorna said, untangling a knot in her beaded necklace. "I'd rather not be sitting there nervous all night, sweating into my new Zac Posen."

"Ew!" Constance whined.

A couple of freshmen at the table next to Josh's cracked up laughing and he lit into them so fiercely they both turned pink in the face. Then he slumped even lower in his chair, yanking his iPod from the pocket of his Easton sweatshirt and jamming the buds into his ears.

"Reed?" Constance asked.

Josh's knee jerked upward so suddenly he knocked over the salt and pepper shakers on his table—which he didn't seem to notice.

"Um, Reed? Hello?" Astrid said.

Lorna leaned across the table and pinched my arm.

"Ow!" I complained, rubbing the spot. "What?"

"What world are you in?" Astrid demanded, staring me down over her laptop screen. "Because I'd like to remember never to visit it."

I sighed, slumping my shoulders forward. "I'm sorry, guys. I'm just really distracted tonight."

"It's okay," Constance said, lifting her coffee to her lips with both hands and blowing across the surface of the liquid. "Everyone's a little stressed right now. Wanna vent?"

"A good venting always works for me," Lorna added.

A heavy feeling flooded my chest, something like gratitude mixed with guilt. Here my friends were, trying to be friends, but I had no interest in telling them what was going on. Because I didn't really understand yet what was going on.

"Thanks, guys, but I think I'm just going to go back to my room and try to get some work done," I told them, getting up and shoving my books into my bag. "Maybe I'll feel better if I can get through some of my to-do list."

"Okay. Well, call us if you need us," Astrid offered.

"I will."

I turned around and started across the crowded, noisy room, leaving my iced tea and any chance I had at a helpful study group behind. But I couldn't do it. I couldn't sit there anymore and stare at my downward-spiraling boyfriend. And I knew that as hard as my friends might try to help me, that was all I'd be doing.

Then, halfway to the door, I paused. Why didn't I just ask Josh what was going on? Ask him if he'd gone off his medication? He was my boyfriend. We were in love with each other. He'd understand that I was just concerned, right? I looked at him over my shoulder and bit my lip.

Or he'd tell me I was crazy, to mind my own freaking business, and bite my head off for basically accusing him of acting like a mental patient.

Screw it. I had to talk to him. I had to put all this uncertainty to rest. I'd taken one step toward him when my phone beeped. I paused with a frustrated groan and yanked it out of my bag.

The noise of the room suddenly quieted to a dull hum in my ears and I paused. The text was from MT.

GET 2 THE CONSTRUCTION SITE. NOW.

I whipped around, my phone clutched in my hand, searching the room. Of course, every other person there was typing on their phone. I tried to stay perfectly still—tried to focus. Suddenly the door near the counter marked STAFF ONLY swung shut. Someone slipped out of the solarium by the side door, which was hardly ever used, and let it slam. And then I saw something partially hidden behind the potted trees near the corner. I took a tentative step back to get a better angle, my pulse racing, expecting to catch a glimpse of blond hair, but it was just a mop and bucket left behind by the janitor. I took a deep breath and tried to calm down, scanning the room once more, but no one was watching me. They were all in their own little worlds. Just like I was in mine. Alone with my mystery texter.

I turned around and headed for the door. Out in the hallway I nearly slammed into Noelle and Ivy, who were locked in an argument.

"You have no idea what you're talking about!" Ivy blurted.

Noelle shoved her hands into her hair. "Oh my God! You weren't even there!"

"Guys?" I said approaching them.

"I didn't need to be there to know what you were doing there!" Ivy replied.

"Guys!" I shouted.

They both clammed up and turned to me.

"What?" they snapped in unison, clearly annoyed at having their latest battle interrupted. But when they saw the look on my face their whole demeanor changed. Ivy's eyes flicked to my phone, still clutched in my hand.

"Reed? What's wrong?" Noelle asked, her brow creased.

Ivy took a step toward me. "Is it—?"

I nodded. "I need you both to come with me," I told them firmly. "Now."

"I can't believe you didn't tell me about this!" Noelle said between gasps as the three of us rushed across campus. The sky above was dark as low clouds crowded out the moon and stars. A chilly wind whipped my hair back from my face.

I glared at her. "First of all, the last time I was getting mystery texts, you and your crazy grandmother were behind them, so—"

"Hey! That's *our* crazy grandmother," she replied, earning a wry laugh from Ivy, who was bringing up the rear. "And this is definitely not her."

"Well, whatever. You've had enough to deal with in the past few months and I didn't want to worry you," I said as the shadowy construction site loomed into view. "Besides, nothing dangerous has happened."

"Except for the whole cement truck thing," Ivy reminded me.

"Yeah, but MT had nothing to do with that," I retorted.

I slowed as the stage I'd stood on just two days ago to cut the cere-
monial ribbon came into clearer focus. The chairs had been removed,
but the podium was still there, and it looked as if someone had hung
something across the front of the wide stage.

"So you think," Noelle said.

Ivy stopped next to us and our ragged breath mingled in the night
as we tried to make out exactly what we were seeing. Finally we were
close enough to read the angry red message that had been hastily
scrawled across the long, white banner.

"Oh my God," I said breathlessly, my hands fluttering up to cover
my mouth.

The banner read: BILLINGS GIRLS ARE MURDERERS! The words were
painted in blood red, the drips and random swipes of the brush making them appear as if they'd been constructed by a madman. Printed
on the banner next to the message were three larger-than-life color
photos. The first was of Ariana Osgood. The next, Sabine DuLac,
who'd killed Cheyenne Martin. And finally, Calista Ryan, Paige and
Daniel's mother.

Okay, so maybe Paige *wasn't* behind all this.

"Those bastards," Noelle said under her breath.

"Who?" Ivy asked. "Do you know who did this?"

"No! I just . . . I just meant whoever did this . . . they're bastards,"
Noelle explained hastily.

"Yeah, and they missed someone," I added angrily. "Where's Mrs.
Kane?" I was surprised by the vehemence behind my words, the force
of the fury rising up in my veins. My eyes blurred with hot tears as the

images from the night of my birthday came flooding back in stark relief. Mrs. Kane practically spitting as she threatened me and my friends. The hateful look in her eyes as the cops dragged her away. The knife flying through the air, straight for my heart. And Mr. Lange. Noelle's father. My father . . . flinging himself in front of me, saving my life, sacrificing his own for mine. The images were so crisp and clear, it was as if the whole thing were happening all over again. I had tried so hard not to think about it for so long, but every last detail had just been percolating in the back of my mind, waiting to burst forth and torture me. "She was a Billings girl, wasn't she? God! If you're going to slander us, at least get all your facts straight!" I shouted, as if anyone near the quad could hear me, as if every one of them was responsible. Something inside of me had broken, and everything I'd been holding inside came gushing out uncontrollably.

"Reed? What're you doing?" Ivy asked shakily as I stomped up the dozen steps to the stage.

"I'm taking it down!" I shouted back angrily. "What does it look like I'm doing?"

The floorboards creaked and bowed beneath my feet as I reached over and yanked at the twine that held the corner of the banner in place. It took a few good jerks, but it came free. Then I stomped over to the center of the banner, which had been secured to the podium. A loud crack sent my heart hurtling into my throat. The raised stage had been hastily constructed and apparently it couldn't withstand my angry tromping. But I was almost done. I got the center of the banner down and moved on to the far side.

"Reed! Wait!" Noelle shouted.

"Get down from there!" Ivy cried.

"Just let me finish!" I yelled back.

I leaned into the railing and reached for the last piece of twine. But as soon as I shifted my weight, the floorboards seemed to fly out from beneath my feet, as if my toes had pushed them in the opposite direction. My stomach swooped end over end as I lost my footing and a loud, wailing groan filled the night air. Ivy screamed, the safety railing collapsed in front of me, and before I could even let out a surprised yelp, I was falling.

FRIEND OR FOE

"Would you believe I've never broken a bone before?" I said, wincing as I opened and closed the fingers on my left hand. The cast was annoyingly pink and impossibly heavy. Ivy had already signed her name in big, elegant letters, and now Noelle was working on her own message. Her long hair grazed the bare part of my arm, just above my elbow, tickling my already itchy skin.

"Really?" she said, her eyebrows popping up. "I always imagined your childhood in West Nowhere, Pennsylvania, to be all swinging from trees and falling off barn roofs."

"Okay, there were no barns in my town. And I wasn't Huck Finn," I told her with a forced laugh. "I was just a tomboy."

"What kind of tomboy never breaks a bone?" Ivy said as she sat in the vinyl chair in the corner of the small, curtained cubicle where we awaited my release forms.

"A careful one, I guess," I said.

"Done." Noelle capped the Sharpie the nurse had left for us and tossed it on the bedside table. I glanced down at the message. It read, *Smooth move, Glass-Licker. xoxo Noelle.*

"Thanks a lot," I said, rolling my eyes.

"That'll just remind you that next time I tell you to stop doing something, you should stop doing it," Noelle warned, crossing her arms over her slim-cut black jacket.

"Noted," I replied.

My phone rang and I glanced warily at my bag. Noelle dug through it until she found my cell and turned the screen in my direction. A picture of Josh smiled lazily out at me.

"Hit ignore," I said without hesitation.

Noelle arched one eyebrow, but did as she was told. She tossed the phone back into my bag and snapped the clasp. "Why are we not telling *le* boyfriend we're in the hospital, exactly?"

Before rushing me to the emergency room, Noelle had told Ivy to call Josh, but I'd shouted at them, through my excruciating, mind-bending pain, not to. Since we were, at the time, limping away from the wreckage of the stage, neither of them asked any questions, but now that I had my stitches—four in the temple, two along the jaw—and my cast, I supposed it was time to fess up.

I looked at my two best friends, the words right at the tip of my tongue. I wanted so badly to talk to someone about this, but I didn't want either of them to be suspicious or scared or even wary of Josh. He was my boyfriend and I loved him. It didn't seem fair to start spouting off about him before I knew what was really going on. I used my thumb to fiddle with my promise ring and cast my eyes down at my lap.

"He's just been really busy and stressed lately and I don't want to make it worse," I said.

"You do know he's going to freak when he sees you and realizes you didn't let him rush to your side all heroic," Ivy said flatly.

I swallowed hard, suddenly recalling vividly how Josh had done just that for Ivy on the night she was shot.

"I know." I picked at the thin bedspread underneath the dirt-stained leg of my jeans. "I'll deal with it. But can we talk about what we really want to talk about here?"

Noelle and Ivy exchanged a knowing glance. "You mean why, exactly, did the stage collapse under you?" Noelle suggested.

"For starters," I said, my pulse skipping ahead as I remembered the awful, swooping sensation of my fall. "Two days ago that thing stood up to the weight of more than a dozen people, but tonight it couldn't handle just me?"

"Well, you *were* going Godzilla all over it," Noelle reminded me, lifting her hair over her shoulder.

"But she does have a point," Ivy said. She narrowed her eyes, leaning forward in her chair. "Did it seem at all unstable on Saturday?"

"No." I shook my head. "I remember a couple of creaky boards, but that's about it."

"So the real question is . . . did someone tamper with it?" Noelle asked, sitting down on the edge of my bed, near my feet. "And if so, who?"

"And what about MT?" Ivy said.

"Exactly," I said, turning up the palm on my good hand. "Did he send me there because he wanted me to find the banner and get rid of it before anyone else saw it, or because he knew the stage was going to cave in and he wanted me to fall?"

All three of us let the words hang in the air as we pondered the question. I felt sick to my stomach from all the uncertainty, all the not-knowing.

"MT . . . friend or foe?" Ivy said, adding a weak, sarcastic laugh.

I wanted to laugh too, but I couldn't make myself do it. I had started to think I could maybe trust my mystery texter. They'd led me to Carolina. They'd let me know—too late, of course, but still—that my room had been violated. But now . . . now I didn't know what to think. Had MT been trying to help me tonight? Or were they trying to kill me?

I stood outside the door to the Art Cemetery on Tuesday night and took a deep breath. Josh was inside, studying in seclusion, and I'd told him I might stop by for a quick break and snack. The moment he'd seen my cast and stitches that morning, he had, as predicted, basically freaked. He was my boyfriend. A girl was supposed to call her boyfriend when she was whisked off to the hospital. But I'd managed to calm him down, telling him I was embarrassed over putting myself in danger and that it wasn't the biggest deal. He'd finally relented, and spent the rest of the day carrying my bag, running to get my food, and opening doors for me, even when it made him late for class.

Yes, he was the best boyfriend ever. And I felt like a disloyal jerk for ever thinking that he might have something to do with the Billings sabotage. Hopefully the chocolate donuts and super-caffeinated coffee would make up for that.

And then, once I had him lulled into a sugar coma, I'd tell him all about MT and the weird stuff that had been going on. He had a right to know.

I held the bag between my cast and my body and lifted my good hand to rap out our secret knock. Three knocks, three knocks, five knocks. Kind of to the beat of *M-I-C . . . K-E-Y . . . M-O-U-S-E*. His idea. I swear.

Josh swung the door open. "Hey!" His dark blond curls stuck up in the front and he had a bit of the crazy professor look about his eyes. He waved me in, peeked out into the hall, then quickly shut the door behind me.

"Everything okay?" I asked.

A quick glance around told me he'd been camping out here a lot lately. The ancient settee where we usually sat and, more often, hooked up, was covered with loose papers, a blanket I recognized from his room, and an Easton Academy hooded sweatshirt. There were a couple of take-out bags on the floor, stuffed with garbage, and My Chemical Romance blasted through the speakers of an iPod dock on the chair in the corner.

"Everything's fine," he said, hastily lowering the volume. "Why wouldn't everything be okay?"

His hands were on his hips, the sleeves of his green rugby shirt pushed up to his elbows. I sat down carefully on the settee and put the bag down on the table next to his open laptop, trying not to disturb the note cards strewn around it.

"No reason," I said. I pressed my lips together and cradled my cast with my other hand. I had to choose my words cautiously here. Clearly he was feeling hyper or tense or both. "Are you going to sit?" I asked, casting my glance down next to me. "I brought your favorites."

Josh tucked his hands under his arms and took a few steps toward the settee, but still kept a good distance. "I just ate, actually, but I'll save them for later. I'm really just wondering what you mean when you ask me if everything's okay."

I blinked. Instantly those nigglings of uncertainty started to bother my nerves again, and the stitches in my chin began to itch. Why was he being so weird? He'd been fine all day, but now he was acting like he'd been chugging Red Bull for the past twenty-four hours.

"I was just asking," I said. "You seem a little tense."

"No, I'm not. Where do you get tense?" he asked, throwing his hands wide. "I'm fine." He walked over to the window and looked out across campus. Then he turned around so suddenly I almost jumped. "Did Graham say something to you?" he demanded. "Or Sawyer?"

I licked my dry lips. Out of nowhere my arm started to throb and then my head began to throb with it. "Something about what?" I asked.

"They did, didn't they?" he said, anger filling his eyes. "God! I should've known."

"Josh, just calm down," I said, standing, still cradling my arm. "I came here tonight to give you a study break. Why don't we just—"

"Calm down?" he said, laughing. "How am I supposed to calm down when my girlfriend, the one person who's supposed to love me no matter what, is talking to other guys about me behind my back?" he blurted. "Especially when one of those guys hates my guts and the other one is clearly totally in love with her?"

I swallowed hard and found myself glancing at the door. This was a Josh I hadn't seen since last year, since the night of his arrest.

"What?" he said. "Aren't you even going to say anything?"

"No, actually," I said, skirting the table and walking steadily toward the door. "I think I'm just gonna go."

"Oh, that's great. That's just perfect," Josh yelled, his green eyes flashing. "Fine! Go ahead and go! Maybe Sawyer's waiting for you back in your room. Maybe you'll talk to him."

"I don't want to talk to him," I said, frustration and anger searing my veins. "I want to talk to you, but you can't even chill out long enough to have a normal conversation." I looked him up and down, my heart cracking slowly. This had not gone as planned. "Maybe when you calm down you can give me a call."

Then I yanked open the door and stormed out, slamming it behind me before he could respond. As I tore across campus, I kept feeling like he was going to come after me, but I refused to look back. I didn't relax until I got to the center of the quad and realized he wasn't going to run up behind me and keep right on yelling. I let out a breath and dropped down on one of the stone benches. I went to hold my head in my hands, but my broken arm protested with an angry, painful twinge and tears filled my eyes. Lovely. I couldn't even properly mope.

"Calm down, calm down, calm down," I told myself, my heel jiggling beneath the bench. I needed to try to look at this whole thing through Josh's eyes. Yes, he'd been acting freakish lately, but did he have a reason? How would I feel if I'd walked in on him, say, holding hands with Ivy? How would I feel if he was in a serious accident and didn't let me know? Maybe he was just reacting the way any normal boyfriend would react when he thought his girlfriend was pulling away.

My teeth clenched and the fingers on my free hand curled around the edge of the bench's seat. This was all Graham's fault. If he hadn't planted those suspicions in my mind, if he hadn't called Josh a liar to my face, I wouldn't be feeling this way. I wouldn't be wondering so much about Josh's mood swings. I would be able to just chalk them up to end-of-the-year stress, separation anxiety, fear of the future.

Wouldn't I?

I let out a groan, tipped my head back, and looked up at the stars in the sky, wishing one of them would bring me some answers. Unfortunately, the stars weren't talking tonight. They simply winked back at me, refusing to tell me who to believe in—refusing to tell me who to trust.

SOMETHING BIG

Even though I knew that watching the clock inevitably made it move slower, I spent the final fifteen minutes of my last class on Wednesday afternoon doing just that. I was supposed to meet Carolina and her camera crew for our first tour of the construction site and I couldn't wait. My last few experiences at the site had been less than positive (understatement of the century), and I was eager to erase them with something good. I figured Carolina's positive energy, and maybe the presence of a camera crew, would frighten off the bad mojo today. Plus, I was dying to see how things were coming along.

Two minutes left to go. As I dragged my gaze away from the clock, it happened to fall on Missy. She was staring at me, her eyes narrowed, and she didn't look away. I swear, it was like giving me the evil eye had become her favorite pastime.

I rolled my eyes at her, just to show her how very unintimidated

I was—even though my heart was now pounding—and pretended to focus on the end of the review.

After what felt like a hundred years, the bell rang and I was out of my seat before anyone else. The door opened just as I got there and I was stunned to find that Josh was the one who had opened it. Instantly, my chest filled with nervous butterflies.

"Hey," I said, averting my eyes.

"Hi." He fell into step with me in the hallway. He was wearing long cargo shorts and a blue crew neck sweater, looking like his normal, yummy self. But I couldn't help remembering his manic body language from last night and the suspicious, slightly crazed look in his eyes.

"Where've you been all day?" I asked, walking quickly toward the end of the hallway.

"I have a paper due tomorrow, so I spent lunch and breakfast in the library," he said, practically chasing me down the stairs. "Are you in a rush for some reason, or are you just that mad at me?"

I sighed half impatiently, half apologetically, as we reached the bottom floor. Josh followed me as I ducked around the corner into a less crowded hallway. I leaned back against the brick wall, adjusting the strap of my bag on my shoulder.

"I have my first tour of the construction site with Carolina," I said, checking my watch. "In about two minutes."

"Oh." Josh looked at his feet. "Okay then. I'll let you go."

A flood of guilt rushed in and drowned all the butterflies in my chest. "No. I mean, it's okay. They can't really start without me. What's up?"

Josh looked up at me through the mop of his hair. "I just feel really bad about last night. I kind of jumped all over you and I didn't mean to."

"It's okay," I said automatically, even as my pride burned at the mention of it.

"No, it's not," he said. "You know it's not." He looked away from me, toward the door and the sunlit quad beyond, as students rushed in and out, widening and thinning the shaft of light at our feet. "I've been so stressed out lately. You wouldn't believe the amount of pressure I've been dealing with. I know it's not an excuse, but it's just . . . the way it is." He met my gaze then, and my pulse skipped a beat. "There's actually something I have to tell you . . . something big." He pressed the heels of his hands into his eyes and took a step back. "But now's not the time. You have somewhere to be."

"Josh. Tell me," I said, reaching for him. I touched his elbow and then my hand fell away, pointless. "I can be late."

"No." He shook his head. "We can talk later. I've been enough of a jerk lately. I don't want to screw this up for you too."

There was a lump in my throat the size of a soccer ball. He looked sad and almost scared, but determined. He wasn't going to tell me his secret. His big thing. Not now anyway. No matter how much I wanted to know.

"Okay," I said. "So . . . call me later?"

He nodded once. "I will."

"Promise?"

"I swear." He crossed his heart with his pinkie.

I turned slowly and headed for the door, giving him all kinds of time to change his mind and stop me, but he didn't. As I made my way outside into the warm sunshine and down the steps of the class building, I felt as if I was going to burst wide open from the pressure of all the questions brewing in my mind. What did he have to tell me? How big was big? Had I been right all along and he was off his meds? Or maybe it was a good thing he had to tell me. Maybe *he* was MT and he had been trying to help me all along. Or maybe it was an even worse thing. Like maybe he was going to break up with me.

I gulped back a bubble of fear as I crossed the quad toward the new Billings. Josh didn't want to screw this up for me by divulging whatever it was that had been bothering him? Well, I had news for him—I had a feeling he'd screwed it up worse by not telling me.

CURSED AGAIN

I tried to forget about Josh as Carolina and I followed Larry around the periphery of the now-finished foundation. It was easier than I thought, putting his aborted announcement out of my head, what with all the construction noise, the sun in my eyes, and Carolina's camera all up in my grill. How she seemed so comfortable with the lens swooping in and out and the boom looming overhead was beyond me. But then, she did do this for a living. I supposed a person could get used to anything.

"I just want you to know, Miss Brennan, that we're looking into the accident with the stage," Larry assured me, walking backward past a couple of guys who were cutting wooden beams with a table saw. "I'm certain it was sound and secure for the ribbon cutting, so I have no clue what could have caused a collapse like that, but we're gonna figure it out and make sure nothing like that happens again."

All around us, construction vehicles ground and squeaked, beeped and churned. A crane lifted a pallet of red and gray bricks, moving them slowly toward what would be the front of the eventual building, while a huge yellow truck backed toward us, carrying piles of two-by-fours. Even with all this activity, I felt perfectly safe—possibly because it was so bright out and I was surrounded by people who knew what they were doing. The camera swung around, taking in all the action, then swung back around to focus on us again.

"Thanks, Larry," I said. Part of me wanted to tell him I was pretty sure that someone other than him and his crew was responsible for the accident—namely Missy Thurber or Paige Ryan—but that would inspire too many questions from both him and Carolina.

"But just so you know, not the smartest idea, climbing around a deserted construction site at night," he told me. I looked up at him and he seemed to suddenly realize that I was, in fact, his employer. He cleared his throat and toyed with his wedding ring. "If you don't mind me saying so, Miss Brennan."

"Trust me, I know," I told him in what I hoped was a comforting voice. I reached into my cast with my fingertips, trying in vain to scratch an itch on my wrist. I was starting to sweat, which was not going to cause good things to happen inside there, I was sure. "I promise I won't be doing that again."

No matter what MT tells me, I added silently.

We had just turned our steps toward one of the half-dozen trucks when I heard a loud and foreboding snap. Larry whirled around, startled, and my heart hit my throat. I automatically looked at the wooden planks beneath my feet, but they were laid on solid ground, only there to keep workers and visitors from tromping over the soil around the foundation too much.

There was another snap. Then a loud shout.

"Watch out!" someone cried.

"Heads up!"

"Get out of there!"

Carolina grabbed my good arm, but for a long moment, neither one of us moved. We had no idea what was happening or which way to go. And then, from the corner of my eye, I saw it. The pallet full of heavy bricks was above our heads, and two of its supports had broken. A third looked stretched to its limits. Two tons of jagged bricks were about to rain down on our heads.

"Run!" I screamed in terror.

The camera lens jerked up to take in the danger. Carolina's eyes widened.

"Run!" she repeated.

Everyone scattered. Carolina, the cameraman, and I ran in one direction. The boom operator tore off in the opposite direction, running after Larry and his assistant. It seemed like only half a second had ticked by before hundreds and hundreds of sharp, heavy bricks rained down in the exact spot where we'd been standing. A huge cloud of dust kicked up, surrounding the area, as half the bricks tumbled over the edge of the foundation and crashed down into what would one day be the Billings basement.

I clung to Carolina as dust and dirt filled my lungs. Both of us had hit our knees in the grass about fifty yards away and we couldn't stop staring at the wreckage. The cameraman, still on his feet, tentatively approached the pile, flinging the lens up toward the now empty pallet suspended high above, down to the pile of bricks, and back up again. All around us, workers shouted to stay back.

"Mike! Don't get too close," Carolina said.

"That was intense," he responded. "We all could have died."

He was practically smiling as he said it. Some kind of death-wish thrill seeker, I guessed. I coughed a few times, trying to dispel the grime from my lungs, as Carolina pushed herself up and dusted off the front of her T-shirt and jeans. She offered me a hand and I took it gratefully. My arm throbbed as if my heart were stuck between my broken bone and my skin.

"Are you okay?" she asked.

"Fine," I replied, glancing up at the torn cords dangling around the pallet. "I think."

Larry jogged toward us, while his assistant shouted at various startled-looking workers, trying to figure out what had happened and who was to blame. I turned in a circle, glancing at all the Easton buildings, at the small klatches of people who had stopped upon hearing the mayhem. I narrowed my eyes, searching their faces, looking for Missy or Paige or that mysterious blond specter I'd seen lurking about—looking for someone who wasn't surprised or who looked disappointed that I hadn't just died.

But all I saw were stunned, wide eyes and pale, frightened faces.

"Are you all right?" Larry asked, grasping Carolina's elbow as he arrived. He was practically doubled over panting and I knew he was more winded from the near-death experience than from the run.

"We're fine," Carolina told him. She tucked a sweaty curl behind her ear and dusted her hands off again with a laugh. "You know, I brushed that reporter off the other day when she asked if this site was cursed, but now I'm starting to wonder," she said jokingly.

Larry laughed as well. As the camera panned to me, I tried to join in, but I found that I just couldn't. Carolina and Larry didn't realize that around here, curses were no laughing matter. Around Easton, and Billings in particular, they were all too real.

DANCE WITH DEATH

"What are we doing up here?" I asked Ivy as we stepped out of the woods into the clearing surrounding the Billings Chapel. The sky was a dark cobalt blue, thanks to a gleaming full moon, and peppered with a million stars. The whitewashed tower of the church rose toward the heavens, looming bright and familiar. We hadn't been to the chapel in months—not since Mr. Lange had died.

"You'll see," Ivy said, drawing her hands up inside the sleeves of her gauzy white sweater. We slowly approached, and she blew into her hands, even though it was a relatively warm night.

"Does Noelle know we're here?" I asked. For the tenth time since we'd left campus and started up the hill, I pulled out my phone and checked it. Josh still hadn't called. He *had* to have heard about my latest brush with death. And even if he hadn't, he'd told me he'd call. He had pinkie-sworn. So where the heck was he?

"She does," Ivy replied, mounting the stone steps. "She kind of invited us."

I blinked, confused, but before I could say anything, she threw open the double oak doors and all my friends jumped out from behind columns and pews.

"Surprise!"

My hand flew to my heart and for a second I thought I was about to find out how it felt to be scared to death. Then I saw the hundreds of candles aglow around the room, the huge banner strung over the pulpit reading, "Congratulations, Reed!" and what seemed to be at least two hundred black and silver balloons cramming the lofty ceilings.

"Congratulations?" I breathed, as Kiki and Lorna swooped in for hugs and Tiffany snapped about a dozen pictures.

"For surviving your latest near-death experience!" Astrid shouted, letting out a celebratory cheer that was echoed by the rest of the group.

I laughed, shaking my head at their ridiculousness as the Twin Cities pulled me into the room. Half the girls were swigging bloodred punch from china cups, the other half toting delicate flutes full of bubbling champagne. "Wow. You really will find any excuse to throw a party."

"You know us *so* well," London chirped. She grabbed a cupcake off a pastry cart at the front of the room and handed it to me. The frosting was green and looked like grass, and a black cookie stuck out from the top with the letters A.R.I.P. piped on in white letters.

"Arip?" I asked.

"Almost Rest In Peace," Portia explained, pointing at each corresponding letter in turn.

I rolled my eyes and handed the cupcake to her. "I'm laughing on the inside," I said wryly. "What else ya got?"

"We have Death by Chocolate, black M&Ms, rocky road ice cream . . . ," Vienna said, walking around the pastry cart and pointing things out like a game-show hostess. "And . . ."

"Our drink choices are Cristal, some crazy blood punch London's brother taught her to make, and . . . Johnnie Walker Black!" Shelby announced, proffering a bottle of scotch. "Want some?"

I laughed and waved her off. "No, thank you. But I *will* have some of that rocky road. . . ."

"Wait! We almost forgot the costumes!" Amberly called out as everyone dug into the desserts. "Where's Noelle?"

"Right here! And no, I don't need any help, thanks for asking," she said, rolling her eyes. She shoved a rolling wardrobe rack out from one of the alcoves on the side of the church, its wheels creaking and squeaking as she tried to maneuver it over the old chipped and warped floorboards. The rack appeared to be packed with black and white clothing, everything from satin to tulle to rubber to spandex.

"Costumes?" I asked warily, sucking the ice cream off an almond before crunching into it. "What kind of costumes?"

"It's up to you," Noelle said, dusting her hands off before leafing through the choices. "You can be the angel of death, a priest, a nun, an assassin, a zombie—a sexy zombie, of course . . ."

"Do they sell any other kind?" Ivy asked, taking a sip from her punch glass.

Already my friends were attacking the rack, always up for a fun wardrobe change. Their chatter filled the room, crowding my chest with its giddy excitement.

"What about this?" Noelle said, emerging from the throng with a grim reaper mask. "I figure the reaper can't come for you if you *are* the reaper."

I put my dish of ice cream aside and plucked the mask from her hands, then sat at the end of the nearest pew, staring down at its gaping eye holes.

"This was your idea?" I asked her.

"I thought I'd take your mind off things without entirely ignoring the unignorable," she said, lifting her palms. "Brilliant, no?"

I tilted my head. "Either that or highly inappropriate."

"Can't it be both?"

Noelle grabbed a black veil from the end of the rack, along with a comically huge black tulle skirt. She shimmied out of her jeans, exposing her string bikini underpants and the scar just above her hip. I felt myself staring at it, as always, and quickly looked away.

"Whoa. What happened to you?" Ivy blurted.

Everyone sort of froze and the conversation died completely. In the two years I'd known Noelle, no one had ever asked her about the scar. I had almost done it a dozen times, but had always stopped myself. Because I thought it would be rude. Or because I didn't want to know. The scar was angry and red and jagged. It just seemed like the story behind that couldn't be anything but bad.

Of course, Ivy had no such concerns.

"Oh, this?" Noelle concaved her stomach and looked down at the scar, running her finger over it. "That was from my own near-death experience."

I swallowed against a dry throat. "When?"

Noelle narrowed her eyes as she stepped into the tulle skirt. "I was, like, seven years old, riding horses with my cousins at my grandmother's ranch—this would be my mom's mom, not *our* grandmother," she clarified. "Anyway, my horse got spooked and threw me and I fell onto an old gardening fork thing that someone had left out."

"Ugh." Amberly stuck out her tongue.

"Gross." London shuddered.

"Yeah. Even grosser? The country hick MD who sewed me up," Noelle said with a wry grimace. "Thus, the scar."

She jammed the black veil down onto her head and flipped the front piece of lace over her face. I stared at her as everyone else got back to dressing.

"That's it?" I said.

She lifted the veil and cocked one eyebrow. "What? You expected something more sinister?"

"Can you blame me? I mean, considering our history . . . ," I said.

Noelle let the veil fall again. "Just goes to show you, Reed. Not everything is part of some big conspiracy." She plucked the mask out of my hands and brought it down over my face. "Some things just . . . happen."

The mask smelled of new rubber and I instantly felt dizzy. But not in an exactly bad way. More like that sugar-high-from-Halloween kind of way.

"Come on," she said, pulling me up by my good arm. "I've always wanted to dance with death."

Someone cranked up the music and Noelle swung me around toward the open area of the church, in front of the first pew. I had a vague inkling that this was somehow sacrilegious, a feeling that only grew as Rose, dressed up as a devil, and Tiffany, decked out as a priest, started twirling around us, holding hands. But considering all I'd been through in the past few days, I decided to just go with it, and within a few minutes I was laughing, relaxing, forgetting.

Maybe Noelle was right. Some things just happened. And even though I didn't exactly believe that my broken arm and my stitches and the broken pallet and the crashing cement truck weren't part of something bigger, tonight I would pretend that I did believe it. Just for my friends. Just for tonight.

My phone beeped in my back pocket and I let go of Noelle to dig it out, figuring it was Josh. But instead it was a text from MT. When I saw the words, my heart all but stopped.

"Is it him?" Noelle asked, looking down over my shoulder.

I took a deep breath and lifted the phone so she could see it better. "Yep."

The text read:

U DON'T WANT 2 GO 2 THE AWARDS BANQUET TMRW. TRUST ME.

CONFESSIONS

"So we're agreed?" Tiffany said as we walked toward the dining hall for breakfast on Thursday morning. "No more putting yourself in mortal peril? At least until *after* graduation?"

I glanced around at her, Portia, Rose, and Ivy and forced a laugh, thinking of MT's latest text and wondering for the millionth time whether I *should*, in fact, trust him. "I'll try."

Ivy gave the others a wry smile, her dark hair falling forward over her sunglasses. "Unfortunately, I think that's the best we're going to get out of her."

The others rolled their eyes collectively. "Fine," Portia said, shrugging her tweed cropped jacket off and hooking it over her arm. It was a warm morning, and everyone on the quad looked like they were already dressing for summer. "But honestly? I think you should have tried to graduate early. You need to get the HOOHFG."

"Whatever that means," Rose joked, nudging Portia with her hip.

We were still laughing when Josh jogged up next to me and joined us. I wasn't sure whether to be happy he was still alive or irritated he hadn't called all night last night.

"Hey," he said, shoving his hands into the pockets of his jeans. "Can I talk to you?"

Finally! I wanted to scream. "Sure." My friends paused in a semi-circle for a moment. "I'll catch up to you guys."

"Fine. But Josh, you keep an eye on her," Tiffany warned, raising a finger and waggling it between us.

Josh's brow knit in confusion, but he nodded. "Okay. I'll do that."

My friends traipsed off and Josh took my hand. "I'm sorry I didn't call you last night. Tiff told me they were taking you out to distract you and I didn't want to interrupt."

"Oh. Well, you could have texted me to tell me that, at least," I said, feeling relieved nonetheless.

"Sorry." Two almost-perfect circles of pink appeared high on his cheeks. "Come on. We need to talk."

"We *so* do."

He tugged me toward the nearest oak tree and tossed his canvas jacket down beneath it for me to sit on. I chuckled at his chivalry, but accepted it. This was one of those rare days when I'd chosen to wear a skirt and I didn't love the idea of twigs and rocks jabbing into my bare skin. I sat down and cradled my cast against my chest, feeling warm and nervous, wondering where this was all going.

Josh sat down next to me and bent his knees, resting his forearms atop them and lacing his fingers together. He blew out a sigh, looked at me sheepishly, and began.

"Okay, here's the thing," he said, chewing on the inside of his cheek. He closed his eyes for a second, like he was building up his confidence. "I wasn't exactly accepted at Cornell."

I blinked. Whatever I had imagined was coming, that wasn't even close. "Wait, you were rejected?"

"Not exactly."

"Then what?" I asked, baffled. Josh had told me back in March that he'd gotten his acceptance letter.

"I was wait-listed," he admitted, ducking his chin. He looked at me from the corner of his eye. "Do you hate me?"

"Hate you? Are you kidding? No!" My voice had gone shrill out of relief. This was so much less bad than anything I had conjured up in my mind. All I wanted to do was get up and do a happy dance. But Josh was not looking quite so elated. "I guess I'm just . . . confused," I told him. "I thought you got in weeks ago."

"I know. I lied," he said, turning slightly toward me. "I'm so sorry, Reed, I was just so embarrassed. My entire family went to Cornell. I mean, everyone except Lynn, but he did get in. I'm the first ever to not get in."

"But you didn't *not* get in," I said. "You got . . . maybe-ed."

"I know. It was just so humiliating. And even worse because . . ."

When he trailed off, my heart thumped fretfully. There was more?

"Because I didn't apply anywhere else."

My jaw dropped.

"I know! I'm such an idiot!" He covered his face with his hands, one of which was peppered with purple paint spots. "I thought it was a lock and I didn't really want to go anywhere else anyway, so—"

"So what you're saying is, as of right now, you don't have a school to go to next year," I clarified slowly. A light breeze rustled the green canopy of leaves over our heads, and I leaned back against the tree's rough bark.

"That's what I'm saying," he replied. "And that's why I've been so stressed. My dad has this friend on the admissions board who basically told him that if I want to get in, I need to get straight As this semester."

Suddenly I felt like the worst girlfriend ever to call herself a girlfriend. Here I was, coming up with all of these disturbing theories, all these scenarios in which Josh was a real villain, while he was fretting about his future and studying his ass off to secure it.

"So that night that I said I was out with Trey, I was actually working with a calc tutor," Josh told me. "And whenever I'm not around, I'm studying."

"Wow," I said.

"And that whole thing with Graham at the library that night?" he said.

My skin prickled with curiosity. "What about it?"

"He and a couple of the other guys found out about the wait-list thing a couple of weeks ago—I don't know how. At first he was just being a dick about it, mocking me for it and crap like that, but that night . . . he actually said that if I didn't break up with you, he was going to tell you about it. Can you believe that?"

"What?" I blurted.

"Yeah. I guess he, like, *really* wants you and Sawyer to get together. Like, badly." He slumped back against the tree as well, tearing up a big chunk of grass and tossing it down in the dirt.

So this was why Graham had called Josh a liar. He knew that he'd lied about getting into Cornell. But why had he made it sound like it was such a huge deal? And what was with the major jones for me to date his brother? Never in my life had I ever heard of a brother who cared *that* much about getting his brother a girl.

"That boy has issues," I concluded quietly.

"Tell me about it," Josh said. "Anyway, that's why I kind of freaked when I saw you with Sawyer that day. After what Graham said . . . I think it just threw me."

"I understand," I told him, reaching for his hand and holding it in my lap. "I just wish you'd told me about all this sooner. I could've helped you study or at least been more understanding about everything."

"I know. I'm an idiot. I was embarrassed," Josh said, tilting his head and giving me a small smile. "Didn't want you to think you were going out with a deadbeat or something."

I laughed and rolled my eyes. "Like I could ever think that."

Josh turned my hand over so my palm was facing up. Gently, he traced the lines of my hand with his fingertip. "So, what's going on with you? It sounded like you wanted to talk about something too."

Josh knew about my latest brush with death, of course, but I'd yet to tell him about MT and the potential connection between the accidents. As he looked into my eyes now, part of me wanted to keep it a secret. Clearly the last thing he needed right now was more stress. But nothing good had ever come of the two of us keeping secrets before. I pressed my lips together and turned toward him fully.

"Promise not to freak out," I said.

"Uh-oh. No good conversation ever started that way," he joked. "What's up?"

So I told him. I told him the whole story of the mystery texter, all the way up to the message I'd received last night to avoid the awards banquet. Josh listened the whole time, his expression growing more and more tense with each passing second. Finally, his knee started to bounce up and down and I had to place my heavy cast on top of it to stop him.

"So? What do you think? Do I trust this person or not?" I asked, really hoping for a definitive answer. For some sort of direction. "Do I say screw it and go to the awards banquet, or do I stay home?"

"First, let me just ask you this," he said. "*How* could you not tell me about this?"

I balked, leaning back. "Okay, pot, go ahead and call me black."

Josh blushed. "Okay, fine, but my secret wasn't potentially life-threatening," he said. He shook his head and looked out across campus. "God, I can't wait to get the eff out of this freaking place. I don't even *care* where I'm going, I just want to get out." Then he looked at me seriously and took both my hands. "I just wish you were coming with me."

"Me too," I said, feeling suddenly, overwhelmingly sad.

Josh looked at me for a long moment, as if trying to see inside, as if gauging exactly what I could handle and what I couldn't. Finally he squeezed my fingers.

"You know what? Screw it," he said with a devil-may-care smile. "We're going to the banquet. You're getting two huge awards and you should be there to accept them. Don't let this latest freak scare you off."

My chest instantly felt ten times lighter, and just like that I knew this was what I'd wanted to hear. "But what if something happens?"

"Nothing's gonna happen," he assured me, looking me in the eye. "I'll make sure it doesn't. I'll get a bunch of the guys together and we'll all be on high alert. No one will be letting you out of their sight."

"Yeah?" I said, raising my eyebrows hopefully.

"I swear," he said, looping his arm around me and pulling me to his side. He kissed the top of my head and held me close. "I won't think about school and you won't think about Billings or this MT nutbag and we'll just have fun."

I narrowed my eyes and tilted my head to look up at him. "Is that even possible around here?"

Josh smirked. "Well, we can at least try."

THE PAYOFF

"Josh is right. You can't just hide out in your dorm room for the rest of your life," Ivy said that afternoon as she pawed through my jewelry box, holding an earring up to her ear, then trying out a necklace. She'd decided she wanted something new to wear with her blue Easton Academy graduation gown, and had apparently chosen to shop for it at the House of Reed. "If there's some kind of threat at the banquet, then we'll deal with it head-on, right? You have to show them you won't be intimidated. That you won't run scared."

"You sound like you're running for Senate or something," I said, looking up from my history textbook. Then I lowered my voice to a deep grumble. "We don't negotiate with terrorists."

"Who knew you could apply that policy at private school?" Ivy smiled as she clasped a beaded necklace around her neck. "Whatever. I'm just trying to get you psyched up." She sat down next to me on my bed and closed my book. "You do know everything's going to be fine, right? Because it is."

"Wow. You are seriously upbeat today," I said, tossing the book aside. "What's your deal?"

Ivy grinned. "I woke up this morning and realized that in one week, I'm graduating. One week and I will never have to sit in one of those awful hard chairs and listen to some obnoxious Easton teacher spout off about something no one in the real world will ever care about. And then I can spend the entire summer looking forward to Pepperdine, looking forward to getting as far away from Easton and Boston and my depressing-ass family as I possibly can, and taking whatever classes I want to take while staring at the Pacific Ocean all day long." She grabbed my arm and shook it. "One more week!"

I groaned out my jealousy and flopped back on my bed. "I'm really starting to think I should have fewer senior friends."

There was a quick rap on my door and it flung right open. I sat up straight in surprise as Carolina rushed in, out of breath, a laptop tucked under her arm and a pencil shoved behind one ear. She looked *Go Green!* camera-ready in a plaid shirt unbuttoned over a lace-trimmed tank top and jeans flared over tan work boots, but the intense vibe she was giving off was definitely not fit for TV. Unless she was guest-starring in a new episode of *Southland*.

"Carolina!" I exclaimed. "What are you doing here?"

"Sorry to interrupt, but you have to see this." She shoved aside my own computer and placed her laptop down on my desk. Ivy and I exchanged a nervous look as we both stood up from the bed and gathered behind her. It took Carolina about thirty seconds to boot up her computer and open up a video screen. "We were going through some of the footage from yesterday, and you're never going to believe what we found."

I gulped back a surge of fear as I leaned in toward the screen. The *Go Green!* trailer appeared in the shot, the logo painted in bright kelly green on the side next to the door. Carolina walked out, talking to the camera. Her lips were moving, but there was no sound.

I reached for the volume button.

"There's no audio on this one," Carolina said. "What I'm saying in this clip is not what matters."

"Carolina, what's going on?" I asked.

Her face was like stone. "You'll see in about five seconds."

On the computer screen Carolina gestured to her right and Mike panned the camera in that direction, taking in the moving construction vehicles, the other trailers, and eventually the foundation of the new Billings. It looked like they were trying to give the viewer a tour of the site—a kind of "before" shot.

"What are we looking for?" Ivy asked, leaning one hand on the desk's surface.

'There!" Carolina hit the space button and the video paused. She pointed at a spot near the top right-hand corner of the screen, her finger trembling. Ivy and I both leaned in as far as we could, but all I could really make out were two people standing close together, one in a hard hat, the other in a straw fedora, and the person in the fedora was handing over a heavy-looking duffel bag. "That's someone paying off one of the workers. The worker who was operating the crane," Carolina said pointedly.

"How do you know there's money in there?" I asked shakily.

"Oh, come on! Just look at it! Haven't you ever seen a spy movie?" Carolina exclaimed, her face reddening. "What else could it be?"

Ivy and I exchanged a dubious look, but said nothing.

"Do you realize what this means?" Carolina continued. "Someone paid him to drop that pallet. Someone was actually trying to kill us. You see it? Do you have any idea who that is?"

I leaned closer. Whoever was handing over the bag was wearing a black trench and jeans. It was obviously a girl, by the short height and the thin waist, but I couldn't make out her face. Still, the idea of a stylish female hanging out around our construction site, handing things off to one of the workers, didn't exactly sit well.

"Hit play," I demanded.

Carolina did. The video kept rolling, and the girl turned away from the camera. There was never a good shot of her face. But as she walked off, I saw something that stopped the breath in my lungs.

"Holy crap," I said under my breath. "Rewind it."

"What? What did you see?" Ivy asked.

My mouth was so dry I could taste my lunch from four hours ago. I reached for the space button and waited. And waited. As soon as the girl started to turn, I hit pause. Now I was certain that Carolina was right—there was money inside that bag, and probably a ton of it.

"There!" I stood up straight and looked at Ivy. "You see her hair? I only know one person with hair like that."

Ivy squinted at the screen, taking in the one, short, silky auburn curl that flew out from under the fedora's brim. Slowly, realization flooded her face and she straightened her posture.

"Who?" Carolina asked, whipping out her phone.

Ivy and I nodded slowly. My blood pulsed in my ears. "That's Paige Ryan."

For once, the arrests weren't made on Easton Academy grounds. The police found the crane operator at his favorite bar. Apparently, Paige had done her research to figure out who would be the most likely crew member to take a payoff, because the guy had immediately and tearfully confessed, saying he needed the money or he was going to lose his house, his family, and pretty much everything else he had in the world. Paige, meanwhile, had been holed up in her parents' vacation home near Mystic, having her feet exfoliated by her personal pedicurist, when the cops came calling. According to my good buddy at the Easton Police Department, Detective Hauer, when she was hauled off for booking, her hair was wet, she had no makeup on, and her toenails were unpolished.

For some reason, this visual made me giddy, no matter how many times I conjured it up.

"What are you smiling about?" Josh asked me, squeezing my hand atop my knee at the Driscoll that night. We were seated at our table in the crowded banquet hall, surrounded by other couples—Astrid and Trey, Kiki and Marc, Noelle and Dash, Ivy and Gage. Well, *they* weren't exactly a couple. Just two people who randomly hooked up whenever it was convenient. But whatever anyone was doing on the side, it was nice to be here among friends. Here and relaxed and out of the danger zone. The bad guy had been arrested, after all. Which meant that whatever MT had been warning me about tonight was not going to happen.

And I was beyond glad about that, because if I'd listened to MT's warning, I wouldn't have been here to accept the junior girls' scholar-athlete award, which I still couldn't believe I'd won.

"Nothing," I said, running my fingers along the gold plate on my plaque, where my name was spelled out in pretty cursive letters. "Just happy to be here."

Josh leaned over and kissed my temple, careful to avoid my stitches. "Me too."

As Headmaster Hathaway presented the junior award for excellence in French, I let my mind wander slightly, looking around the room at all the proud senior-class parents, the texting classmates, the hustling waiters. Kiran and Taylor were both there, sitting near the windows with some random, hot alumni fawning all over them. After the banquet we were all going back to Noelle's room for an old-school-style Billings celebration. This night that I had been dreading all day was going to end up being beyond cool.

I did, of course, still have my questions for Paige Ryan. Like, why?

Why was she trying to kill me? Was she just trying to finish the job her mother had begun down in St. Barths over Christmas break? Did she want to be the one who got to rebuild Billings so badly that she'd actually commit murder? Did she still hate me for hooking up with Upton Giles that week? Or did she hate me because, in some twisted way, she blamed me for the fact that her mother was in jail? Then there was the off chance that she actually subscribed to all that Billings curse mumbo jumbo Mrs. Kane had been spouting before she was arrested back in March. Maybe she thought I needed to die in order for Billings to live on free of bad luck.

Any way you sliced it, the girl was mad crazy.

"And now for the awards for overall academic achievement in the junior class," Headmaster Hathaway announced. I sat up a bit straighter, my heart prickling with nerves. Now that I had won scholar-athlete, I knew I had a shot at snagging this one as well, and I was beyond proud of myself for managing to get good grades this year even with all the insanity that had gone on. "As with the freshman and sophomore classes, this award is given out to one female student and one male student—the two students who have achieved the highest GPAs for the first three quarters of the year. And those students are . . . Reed Brennan and Sawyer Hathaway!"

Josh's face lit up as my heart all but burst. He gave me a quick kiss and a hug. "I'm not worthy," he joked as the room filled with applause.

"What?" Marc blurted under his breath. "Sawyer wasn't even here the first half of the year."

"They used his grades from his last school," Noelle explained.

Marc slumped, blowing out an annoyed breath. "Please. This is nepotism at its finest."

Everyone laughed and Josh squeezed my hand one more time before I got up to accept the award. I smiled and smoothed out the full skirt of my blue silk Chloé dress, scanning the room for Sawyer. His father looked out at the crowd as well, applauding along with the audience, but Sawyer didn't appear. As the moments passed, a crease of confusion deepened just above the headmaster's nose. Everyone was looking at me, so I made my way up to the podium to collect my second plaque and gift certificate. It took a couple of minutes for me to weave around all the tables and chairs, but still, no Sawyer.

"Well," the headmaster said, leaning toward the microphone. "I guess I'll have to give my son a little talking-to later."

The crowd responded with polite laughter and Headmaster Hathaway turned his attention to me.

"Congratulations, Miss Brennan."

"Thanks," I replied.

He handed over the prizes and shook my hand. We posed for the requisite photo, and then I was done. On my way back to my chair, Noelle shot me a bemused look and I shrugged. We both knew it wasn't like Sawyer to miss something like this. He loved school almost as much as Noelle loved Calvin Klein.

"What happened to your partner in brilliance?" Josh joked as I sat down next to him, tucking the plaque under my chair.

"I don't know. Now that I think about it, I don't think he was in class all day. Maybe he's sick."

"But then wouldn't his own father know about it?" Astrid asked, taking a sip from her water goblet.

A slight tickle of foreboding skittered down my neck. I reached for my bag and pulled out my phone.

"What're you doing?" Josh asked.

"Texting him," I replied.

I knew Josh wasn't Sawyer's biggest fan at the moment, but I'd hoped we'd cleared up the facts that (a) I wasn't interested in Sawyer in a boyfriendly way, but (b) he *was* my friend. I typed a quick message and hit send, then left my phone on the table between my silver knife and Josh's salad plate to wait for his response.

Forty-five minutes and ten awards later, he still hadn't written back. Finally, the seniors were done being honored, and the awards part of the evening was over.

"Let's have one last round of applause for all our honorees!" Mr. Hathaway announced as he finished his closing speech. The resounding cheers were so loud a few people actually laughed in surprise. "And now, go ahead and enjoy your meals! Thank you all for coming!"

Almost instantly, waiters scurried to deliver the main course. A few people got up from their seats to stretch their legs and visit other tables.

"I'm gonna go hit the bathroom," Josh said, giving me a quick peck on the cheek. "Be right back."

"I'll just be here devouring this salmon," I replied.

He and Trey headed off for the bathroom while Gage started to nuzzle Ivy's ear, making her giggle. Noelle rolled her eyes in disgust and dragged Dash off to go say hello to some alumni. As the rest of us dug into our food, I saw Missy Thurber, of all people, winding her way around the many tables as if headed for ours. I was even more surprised when she walked all the way around until she was right behind me.

"I hope you're proud of yourself," she said, pressing her hands into the back of Josh's vacated chair. I almost choked on my food. So she was actually talking to me now? Our relationship was no longer going to exclusively consist of evil glares?

"Proud of myself?" I asked.

"You seem to be picking off the Billings alums one by one," she said, looking me up and down in an obnoxious way. "Guess I should stay away from you. Who knows what lies you'll come up with about me to get me sent to jail?"

Astrid let out an indignant grunt. "Back off, you troll. Reed hasn't lied about anyone."

"You do know there's actual proof that Paige paid off some guy to kill me and Carolina," I said, turning in my seat to face her. "The guy confessed."

Missy laughed. "Proof. Ha. Everything can be doctored these days, Reed. I'll bet you a million dollars that video gets thrown out before it even makes it to court. And that guy was drunk when he blabbed. No one's going to believe a loser like him over Paige Ryan." She stood up straight and squared her shoulders, looking right into my eyes. "Either way, don't think for a second that this is over," she said through her teeth.

Then she reached over, plucked the fresh, warm roll from my bread plate, and took a bite out of it before walking off.

I gaped at Astrid, stunned.

"Did she really just steal your bread?" she asked.

"I think she really just did," I replied.

And we both cracked up laughing. Honestly, when it came to villainous behavior, Missy had some brushing up to do. But still, something inside of me stirred. What did she mean, this wasn't over? Did she have something to do with all these "accidents" too? Had she been working with Paige? They were cousins, after all, and Missy had hated me since our first day of sophomore year.

I watched her carefully as she crossed the room and sauntered over to Graham Hathaway. She ran her hand lightly over his shoulders, then picked up her clutch purse from his table and disappeared out a side door. It was a side door I knew all too well. I'd met Dash McCafferty in a little alcove through there last fall for one of those stolen moments between the two of us that I wasn't too proud of. Graham took a last bite of potatoes and got up to follow her, buttoning his blue suit jacket as he went.

I watched the door swing shut behind them, then pushed my chair away from the table.

"I'll be right back," I said to Astrid.

I grabbed my phone and took off after them.

NOT AGAIN

I crept around the corner and into the small alcove and almost lost my two bites of salmon. Graham had his tongue so far down Missy's throat he could probably taste that roll she'd snagged from me moments ago. Her back was mashed up against the wall and his whole body was flattened against her even as he tried to wiggle his hands between their chests to get a feel.

Okay, ew. I had to look away. This wasn't right. But I couldn't seem to make myself move. It was like watching a truly horrible *American Idol* audition. You felt for the poor sap crooning away, so off-key he could shatter glass; you felt for the judges as they tried in vain to stop cringing; the whole thing made you feel queasy inside, but for some sadistic reason you had to see it through to the bitter end.

Missy turned her face, smearing her lipstick across her cheek, and started to open her eyes. A sudden surge of panic hit me hard, and I was about to turn away before she could accuse me of being a creeper, but I was too late. She looked right at me, blinked, and then I swear she started to smile.

I turned, my heel catching on the ornate hallway rug, and stumbled around the corner. At that moment, someone's gloved hand came down over my mouth and a strong arm locked around my waist. My heart hurtled into my throat and I tried to scream, but the fingers were clamped down too tightly against my lips as I was pulled roughly backward. I flailed and kicked and writhed, but nothing worked. My good arm flung out as my attacker dragged me toward the end of the hallway and for a brief, desperate second I was able to clasp the corner between the alcove and the hall, but with one jerk the guy freed my grip and we were all alone.

We were headed toward a back exit. A door that I knew led to the employee parking lot, which would be all but deserted, what with everyone working the banquet. My eyes filled with hot, angry, frantic tears.

This was not going to happen to me. Not again. Not without a fight. I whacked at my attacker with my cast as hard as I could and felt his grip give the tiniest bit. At that moment, Josh, Trey, and Gage came running into the hall. My eyes widened with hope as Josh turned and saw us.

"Hey! What the hell are you doing?"

The guys sprinted toward me and my attacker let go, dropping me on my ass in the center of the hall. He turned and fled out the back door. Gage and Trey went gunning right past me and gave chase. Josh ran over and fell to his knees in front of me.

"Are you all right?" he asked, running his hand over my forehead and into my hair. "Who the hell was that?"

"You didn't see his face?" I gasped, clinging to my broken arm, which radiated sharp pains up into my shoulder and down into my fingertips.

Josh shook his head. "He was wearing a ski mask."

"Oh my God." I leaned into Josh's chest, my breath coming short and ragged as wave after wave of terror crashed over me. "I thought it was over. Paige is in jail . . . I thought . . . I thought I was safe."

"I know." Josh ran his hand over my hair again and again and kissed the top of my head. "I know. It's okay. We got here in time. Everything's gonna be okay."

Suddenly Gage and Trey reappeared at the back door. They were out of breath and soaking wet. Apparently the skies, which had been threatening since that afternoon, had finally opened up. Gage doubled over as he clung to the door handle and I saw lightning flash through the sky behind him. He finally straightened up and let the door slam.

"Anything?" Josh asked.

"He took off in a black Acura," Trey said as he fought for breath. He ran his hand over his close-shaven head, sloughing off the rain. "I tried to get the plates, but I only saw the first two letters."

"Well, at least that's something," Josh said. He tipped my face up with his finger beneath my chin. "We should go to the police."

I shook my head, tears streaming from the corners of my eyes. I felt like an idiot for going off on my own. For thinking this was over just because Paige was locked up. For not listening to MT. "I just want to go home."

"But we have to report this," Josh told me.

"So let them come to me for once," I said, bracing my hand against the wall and struggling to my feet. All three of the guys—even Gage— made a move to help me, but I managed to do it myself. "Right now all I want to do is lock myself up in my room. And until someone figures out what the hell is going on around here, I'm not coming out."

"So let me see if I understand all this," Taylor said later that evening, pacing back and forth in front of my closet. Outside my window at Pemberly the storm raged, thunder growling and lightning flashing. The rain pelted the windowpane, sometimes so loudly it drowned out our words. Every now and then the lights would flicker and I just prayed we wouldn't be left in the dark. That was the last thing my nerves needed right now. "This Sabine girl totally screwed with your mind via e-mail and text, then Noelle and her grandmother totally screwed with your mind via e-mail and text—"

"Um, hello? Sitting right here?" Noelle said, raising her hand from my desk chair like she was going to ask a question in class.

Taylor shot her a look that said "Let me finish." Wow. Things had really changed.

"And now this MT person is screwing with you via text?" she finished.

"That's the deal, basically, yeah," I replied, leaning back into my pillows, which were propped up against the wall at the head of my bed.

I'd changed into my favorite Penn State sweatshirt and Easton soccer shorts upon returning to the dorm, and had just finished giving my statement about tonight's incident to Detective Hauer, who had left with a promise to run the partial plate against the car's make as soon as he got back to the Easton PD. While part of me would have loved to pass out and put this night behind me, I was far too wired to sleep, which was why everyone was here, keeping me company. Kiran leaned back against the door and Ivy sat at the foot of my bed, her back against the wall and her feet dangling over the edge of the mattress.

"Reed, I think you know what you need to do," Taylor said seriously, crossing her arms over her chest. "You need to give up on technology."

I snorted a laugh.

"She's right," Kiran put in, inspecting her fingernails. "Technology is not your friend." Her eyes lit up and she pushed herself away from the wall. "Maybe you should move to, like, the African jungle or something. Become one of those women who lives off the land and studies the apes or something. Go completely off the grid."

A bolt of lightning flashed so brilliantly I nearly jumped out of my skin. Taylor smirked and walked over to my dresser, piling her hair atop her head and checking out the effect in the mirror. While Ivy, Noelle, and I had gone casual, she and Kiran were still sporting their cocktail dresses, having come right back here with us instead of stopping by their rooms at the Driscoll.

"Yes, Kiran. That is *so* what I want to do with my life," I said sarcastically as the thunder clapped just outside. "Why didn't I think of that
before?"

"Besides, we already decided. No running and hiding," Ivy
reminded me.

"So if we're not gonna run and hide, I say we go on offense,"
Noelle said, leaning forward in the chair. "Find out who this MT
person is already and grill them about what they actually know until
they snap."

"But there's no way to find out," I told her, supporting my cast
with my other hand. "Every time we try to text them it bumps back to
me as unsent."

"Oh, please. They're probably just blocking you," Taylor said, letting her hair tumble down around her shoulders again. "Any good
hacker can get around that."

I looked at Ivy and she sat up straight, pushing away from the wall.
"Any good hacker?" I said. "Aren't you a good hacker?"

"How?" Ivy asked Taylor. "We tried texting and calling from my
phone—"

"And mine," Noelle said.

"But they came back too."

"You just have to set up a program to run the numbers," Taylor
said, lifting a palm as if it was the most obvious thing in the world.
"There's no way this person blocked every sequence. We find the
right sequence, reprogram one of our phones, and we're in."

Ivy's jaw snapped shut and she brought her hand to her forehead.

"Why didn't I think of that?" She shoved herself off the bed and grabbed her phone from on top of my dresser. "We'll start with the most obscure area codes first."

"Good call," Taylor said.

Ivy started typing into her phone as Taylor leaned over her shoulder. Before long the two of them were whispering and pointing, debating and correcting. I glanced at Kiran and she shrugged in response.

"Got any good magazines?" she asked, dropping down next to me on my bed. "This could be a while."

"Please. She gets *Shape* and *Fitness* and nothing else," Noelle said, rising from her chair. "I'll be right back."

An hour later Kiran, Noelle, and I were noshing on Godiva and pawing through the latest issues of *Vogue*, *InStyle*, and *W*, while Ivy and Taylor sat on the floor bent over Ivy's phone. It wasn't exactly the party we had originally planned for the evening, but it was darn close, and they were all there with me, which was the best gift I could have asked for. The thunderstorm had passed and the rain had let up a bit, dulling itself to a persistent drizzle, the sound of which was far more comforting than the raging we'd endured earlier. Suddenly Ivy leaned back on her hands, a self-satisfied smile on her face.

"And . . . done!" she announced.

"Done?" I asked dropping the heavy *Vogue* issue aside. "You got through?"

"Yep," Taylor said happily.

"Finally," Kiran groused.

"What did you say?" I asked, getting up from the bed and wiping my palms on the back of my sweatpants.

"We wrote, 'Enough with the mystery. I want to know what's going on. We need to meet,'" Taylor replied.

"To the point," Noelle conceded, tipping her head.

"Do you think he'll write back?" Kiran asked, sipping bottled water through a straw.

I sighed. "We'll just have to wait and—"

Ivy's phone beeped. My heart dropped. We all froze.

"Is it MT?" I asked.

Ivy hit a button and nodded, as Taylor leaned in so close her hair fell over Ivy's shoulder. "It says, 'Come alone. One hour. Directions attached.'"

"Holy crap," I said, a rush of excitement flooding my veins. "It worked."

"Come alone. Yeah. Like that's gonna happen," Noelle said, lifting her thick hair over her shoulder.

"We're going with her?" Kiran asked, a tad fretful.

"Of course we are," Ivy snapped.

"Don't worry, Kiran. MT has proven he . . . or she . . . is a friend," I assured her.

"Then why does he want you to come alone?" Taylor asked. "What's with the blocking the number and all the mystery?"

"Well, clearly he's trying to protect himself," Ivy replied. "Whoever's after Reed means business if they're going to try to kid-nap her from a crowded event."

Kiran bit her lip. "Yeah, but—"

"All right, enough," Noelle snapped. "We're all doing this together. There's safety in numbers right? If we all go together, everything will be fine."

The five of us looked around at one another and I felt this odd mixture of fear and hope. By the end of tonight, I might know who MT was, and I might even know everything he or she knew about this latest attack. But I also knew that ventures like this one didn't always end up the way I expected. And sometimes they didn't end well at all.

SPY-FABULOUS

"I don't like this," Josh said, standing in the center of Ketlar Hall's common room. All along the walls, guys were hunched over their computers at the study carrels, typing furiously or reading over papers and notes. The couches and chairs were laden with last-minute crammers, trying to get in every minute of good study time before tomorrow morning's exams. Everyone had changed out of their suits and ties and into worn T-shirts and comfy shorts, and there were bags of junk food and cans of energy drinks and soda everywhere. Suddenly I felt very lucky to not have a final at 8 A.M. tomorrow. "What happened to locking yourself in your room and not coming out?"

"I know," I said. "But this texter person isn't the enemy. Think about it. He warned me not to go tonight, and he was right. I shouldn't have gone."

"Okay, well, if he's such a friend, then why are you bringing along Charlie's Angels over there?" He lifted his chin toward the doorway, where Ivy and Noelle loitered, ignoring each other and waiting for me. They did look sort of spy-fabulous in dark jeans, heeled boots, and black jackets. A dripping and colorful Coach-logo umbrella dangled from Ivy's wrist, while Noelle had propped her plain black version against the wall.

"Because they have nothing better to do?" I suggested, lifting one shoulder.

"I should come with you," Josh said, reaching for my hand.

"No way. You have to ace AP bio tomorrow," I reminded him, as if he needed reminding. "I'm not gonna let you screw up your entire future just to do this with me. Especially when I already have enough backup."

"Backup? Sure." He scoffed. "What are they going to do if you get jumped again, whip out a nail file?"

I leveled him with a glare. "Would you want to go up against Ivy and Noelle when they're pissed off?" He sort of gulped and paled and I had my answer. "Besides, Kiran has a stun gun. She went back to her hotel to grab it and change her clothes."

"She has a stun gun?" Josh asked, his eyebrows popping up.

"She said it's just good sense when you're a high-fashion model," I replied. "Apparently, the guys in Italy are all about the groping."

Josh was silent for a moment, pondering. Then he dropped my hand and groaned in frustration, plopping down on the nearest leather couch. He blew out a sigh and looked up at me imploringly.

"Are you sure you don't want to just go to the police with this?" Josh asked, extricating his phone from the pocket of his cargo shorts. I'd forwarded him the text with the attachment and he still had it up on his screen. "Give them the directions and let them figure it out?"

I sat down next to him and knocked the side of my knee against his. "How about this? If you don't hear from me in two hours, send in the SWAT team, the dogs, the helicopters. Whatever."

Josh knocked his fist against his mouth a few times but finally gave in. "Okay, fine. It's a plan."

I threw my one good arm around him and squeezed. And even though I hadn't exactly come here for his permission, I whispered a quick "Thank you," because it was important to me that he believed in me and wouldn't be sitting here terrified the whole time I was gone. Then I kissed him and got up, my ponytail swinging behind me. Josh rose as well, turning to watch as I joined my friends at the door.

"Ready?" Noelle asked, glancing at her phone to check the time.

"Ready."

"Hey, guys?" Josh called out in full voice, earning some annoyed glances from the studying hordes around him.

"Yeah?" Ivy said.

"Take care of her, okay?" Josh told them.

I wasn't sure whether I should be offended that he thought I couldn't handle myself, or pleased that he cared. But then, I supposed

I did have a broken bone and a track record for getting into trouble, so I kept my mouth shut.

Noelle, meanwhile, looped her arm over my shoulders and squeezed. "Always do."

DÉJÀ VU

"Raccoon!" Taylor shouted, pointing toward the windshield from the center seat in the back of Kiran's rented Escalade. Noelle slammed on the brakes and we were all flung forward for a second before the massive SUV came to a complete stop, its tires squealing on the wet pavement. My hand flew to my heart as the raccoon paused for a moment, gave us a withering stare, and continued loping across the road.

"Okay, *why* are you driving my car again?" Kiran demanded, glaring at Noelle from the front passenger seat.

"Because my car was too small and we all know your driving's for shit," Noelle replied, slowly rolling ahead again. The windshield wipers thwapped violently back and forth, sending sprays of water into the night with each giant arc.

"Yeah. And clearly you're way better," Kiran complained, resting her elbow against the top of her door and her head on her hand.

"Well, maybe if any of these damn streets had streetlights," Noelle shot back.

"Guys. Can we stop sniping for a second and focus?" I asked, gripping the back of Kiran's seat with my free hand. "Where are we?"

"We have to take the next left," Ivy said, her phone aglow in her lap, casting a white light over her already pale features.

"Does anyone *see* a next left?" I asked, squinting into the night.

"There!" Kiran pointed at a street sign that was half hidden by a low-hanging tree branch. Noelle cut the wheel and we all screeched as the car skidded around the corner, veering into the far lane.

"Next time, *I* drive," Ivy muttered, her hand braced against the window.

This road was even scrawnier than the last, and clouds of fog rose up from the pavement, gathering around the car as we cut through. I turned and gazed out the window to my right, trying to see anything in the dark—a house, a business, a barn, a gas station—but all I saw were trees, trees, and more trees. An ancient but well-maintained stone wall loomed into view, terminating at the base of a driveway with a tall iron gate. The house beyond wasn't visible from the road, either because of the fog or because the driveway was so long, the house was hidden by trees.

Taylor glanced past me, then did a double take when she saw the gates. She leaned toward the window, crushing my cast, and I let out an involuntary gasp.

"Oh God! Sorry," Taylor said, sitting up straight again. "But, you guys, do you realize where we are right now?"

"The middle of nowhere?" Kiran theorized.

"Trapped in some bad horror movie?" Ivy joked as the fog thickened.

"I think both," Taylor said, looking skittish.

"What do you mean?" I asked, all the little hairs on my arms standing on end.

"It says to take the next right, just after the covered bridge," Ivy announced. Then she looked up from the page. "Wait a second. The covered bridge?"

While her words still hung in the air, the structure appeared as if from nowhere, and the Escalade's tires bumped and thumped over its old creaky boards. For a moment, we were eerily cut off from the outside world, the noise of the rain stopped, and all I could hear was the sound of our breathing and the squealing of the suddenly dry windshield wipers. I had this sinking sense of déjà vu as the car reemerged into the rain and Noelle slowed to make the turn.

Seconds later my throat went dry and Noelle hit the brakes. I held my breath. No one moved. Rising up out of the fog at the top of the hill were the uppermost floors of a house I knew all too well. A house I hadn't stepped foot inside for more than a year. A house I had visited on one of the most horrific nights of my life.

Kiran clutched the door handle, as if ready to bolt. "Isn't this—?"

"Yeah, it is," Noelle confirmed. "It's Cheyenne's house."

The very house my friends and I had partied and laughed and played dress up in on the night Ariana Osgood had attempted to kill me.

FINISH THE JOB

"Turn off the lights!" I whisper-shouted at Noelle.

"What?" she asked.

"Turn off the lights and pull over! Now!" I cried.

My chest constricted and I doubled over in my seat, gasping for air. Noelle shot me a disturbed look and did as she was told. I pressed my forehead into the back of Kiran's leather seat and told myself to chill. Told myself to breathe. But I couldn't seem to make it happen.

All I could see were flashes of blond hair. All I could hear was that evil snicker. Someone had been watching me this past week. I had felt it. I had *sensed* it. And now I knew exactly who that someone was.

"Reed? Are you okay?" Ivy asked.

I could hear myself gasping hoarsely. My throat and lungs burned. My heart pounded so hard I could feel it in my skull. I was going to pass out, and the very thought terrified me even more.

"I think she's having a panic attack," Taylor said, putting her hand on my back. "Roll down the windows."

"But it's pouring rain," Kiran whined.

"She needs air!" Ivy shouted.

All four windows rolled down. The side of my face and my arm were peppered with cold, wet droplets of rain and cool air flooded my skin.

"Concentrate, Reed," Taylor instructed, her voice soothing. "Try to breathe."

I can't! my brain wailed. *Ican'tIcan'tIcan't.*

But I had to. I closed my eyes, clamped my mouth shut, and pulled in a breath through my nose, which made me cough. But still, it was something. I forced myself to concentrate and tried again. I breathed in through my nose and out through my mouth.

In and out. In and out. In and out.

Finally, I was able to sit up again.

"Are you okay?" Taylor asked.

"I think so." I shot her a weak but grateful smile. "Thanks."

"What the hell just happened?" Noelle asked, one hand still gripping the wheel. "Where did that come from?"

"It's Ariana," I said, my voice breaking. "She's behind this. This is all one big game and she's trying to lure me here so she can finish me off."

"Reed, Ariana's locked up. She doesn't even have access to a cell phone," Noelle reminded me.

I shook my head violently, desperation coursing through my veins, swelling my heart. "It's her. I know it's her. She's gotten out somehow and she's trying to kill me. I just know it."

"Reed, calm down," Taylor said, rubbing my back. "If Ariana had broken out of prison somehow—"

"Which is highly unlikely as she is the least athletic person I know," Noelle said.

"—then we would have heard about it," Taylor finished.

"But what if we didn't?" I asked. "I know you guys are going to think I'm crazy, but someone's been spying on me on campus the past couple of weeks. I keep feeling someone watching me, and every time I look there's someone disappearing around a corner or into a building, but I always catch a glimpse of blond hair."

"So maybe it was Missy," Ivy suggested. "I wouldn't put it past her to eff with you just for kicks."

"It wasn't," I insisted. "It was—"

"Not Ariana," Noelle said fiercely.

"But what if it *was*?" I snapped through my teeth.

At that moment my phone beeped and we all screamed. Which actually made me feel better. Momentarily. Until I looked down at the screen. I read the text aloud.

LEAVE CAR WHERE IT IS & WALK THE REST. KEEP 2 THE TREES UNTIL U GET 2 PATH THRU BACK GARDEN. OH & LEAVE UR LITTLE FRIENDS WHERE THEY R, RULEBREAKER.

"Omigod it's totally her," I whimpered.

"It's not!" Noelle replied. "And there's no way we're staying here."

"Are you sure about that?" Kiran asked tentatively. "I mean, the instructions say—"

"No. We're going," Ivy put in, shoving her own phone into the pocket of her jacket. "There's no way Reed's going in there alone."

"I don't even want to go in," I replied, my voice shrill. "I say we go with Josh's plan. Call the police and let them deal with it."

"But if we call the police, MT might bolt and then we'll never know what's going on," Ivy said, leaning forward in her seat to see me better. "Come on. There's safety in numbers. We'll be fine."

"I don't know, you guys," Kiran said, looking up at the fog-obscured house. "This is all a little too *Scream* for my tastes."

"That's it," I said. "I'm calling the police."

"What're you going to say?" Ivy asked. "That we followed an anonymous texter's directions into the middle of nowhere and now we're scared? They'll laugh in your face."

"No, they won't. Detective Hauer knows me," I said, hitting the speed dial button. "It'll be fine."

The phone rang only once before he picked up.

"Detective Hauer," he barked.

"Detective? It's Reed Brennan," I said, clutching the phone to my ear.

"Reed?" He sounded alarmed. Which made sense. When had I ever called him with *good* news? "Is everything all right?"

"Not exactly. I'm out at Cheyenne Martin's house, the one on Old Post Road? And I'm pretty sure Ariana Osgood is here," I said.

In the front seat Noelle hung her head into her hand. On the other end of the line, I heard phones ringing and a door slam, but otherwise, there was silence.

"Detective?"

"I'm sorry. I'm waiting for the punch line," Detective Hauer said.

I gritted my teeth. "I know it sounds crazy, but—"

"Reed, I don't even know where to start," the detective said with a heavy sigh. "Why in hell would you be out at the Martin place on a night like this after what happened to you earlier this evening? And what in God's name would make you think that Ariana Osgood is there when we both know she's locked up safe and secure in Virginia?"

Okay. Clearly I shouldn't have led with the Ariana thing. My brain whirled, trying to figure out how to backtrack, where to start, how to make him believe me.

"I know, but I—"

"No. You know what? I don't have time for this," he said, his voice quickly growing gruff. "I'm too busy filling out the paperwork your last call generated, not to mention interviewing attempted-murder suspects and dealing with their highly irritating New York lawyers."

"But that's—"

"Reed, I seriously think you should consider the possibility that you might have a slight addiction to drama, both real and imagined," the detective said. "If Ariana Osgood jumps out from behind a pillar and tries to whack you, give me a call."

And the line went dead.

"What'd he say?" Taylor asked.

I was too humiliated to repeat even half of it. I shoved my phone back in my pocket and sighed resignedly. "He said we're on our own."

Everyone slumped. I stared down at my hands, feeling seriously deserted.

"It's not Ariana, Reed," Noelle said in a reassuring tone. "I guarantee you it's not."

"She's right. I mean, it's just not possible," Taylor said. "If she'd gotten out somehow, we would know about it."

"Taylor?" Noelle said, angling further in her seat. "You haven't said what you think we should do."

Taylor slowly looked around at each of us, kneading the knees of her skinny, black chinos in her hands. She bit her lip, screwing her lips up in anguished thought.

"I say we go in," she said finally. "But Reed and Kiran can stay here if they want."

"Yes!" Kiran cheered, pumping a fist by her side. "You three have fun!"

"No. No way. I'm not letting you guys go without me," I said, reaching for the door handle. "If you're all going, then I'll go too."

"Good. Then it's settled," Noelle said, popping her door open. "We'll all go and Kiran the cowardly supermodel will stay here."

"By myself?" Kiran squeaked.

"Your choice," Noelle said with a shrug.

Kiran hesitated. The four of us stared her down as we waited for her to make a decision. Finally, with a heaving sigh, she drew her stun gun out of her pocket. It was about the size of an iPhone, and when she hit the button to test it, a sizzle of blue light appeared between the two wires, releasing a comforting electric crackle. I just hoped Kiran's reflexes were fast enough if Ariana jumped out from behind a curtain and tried to slice and dice me.

"All right," she said resolutely. "I'm in."

LIFE'S LITTLE SURPRISES

We didn't bring the umbrellas. Big mistake. Within five minutes of walking I was soaked through, my hair dripping ice-cold water down my back, and as hard as I tried to shield my cast from the rain, it was getting wet too. I tried not to think about what the consequences of that might be as my feet sunk into the two inches of mud along the side of the road, making awful sucking sounds each time I lifted them.

Noelle tucked her sopping wet hair behind her ears, then held back a low-hanging branch and waited for us to pass her by.

"So much for these shoes," Kiran groused, teetering along in her heeled boots. "My stylist is *not* going to be happy with me."

"You should've worn sneakers," Noelle admonished at a whisper. The rest of us had changed into loose black sweatshirts and running shoes, while Kiran had insisted on going designer-chic.

"Well, I didn't know we were going on a wilderness hike, did

I?" Kiran demanded. "God. This MT couldn't have just met us at a Starbucks like a normal human being?"

For a moment I swear Noelle considered letting the branch snap back in Kiran's face, but thankfully she restrained herself. As we neared the house, the wind kicked up, howling through the woods around us and turning the wet leaves on the trees upside down. A low rumble of thunder sounded in the distance. I stopped in my tracks, blinking the rain off my lashes as I looked up at the turrets of the house. With its gargoyle details, the rain pouring off the eaves, and the dozens of windows shuttered and curtained, it looked like something out of a nightmare.

"Are we sure about this?" Taylor asked.

"Let's just get it over with," Noelle said, tromping ahead.

We all exchanged wary looks but followed. It was, after all, what we did—followed Noelle. Except for Ivy. I wasn't exactly sure what she was still doing here, unless it was due to our friendship, or perhaps her own morbid curiosity. She and Cheyenne had, at one time, been best friends, but I was sure she hadn't been back to this house in years.

"Where exactly are we going?" Kiran asked as we came up even with the side of the house. It seemed like most of the curtains were drawn on the first floor as well, and there wasn't a light to be seen. If MT was in there somewhere, he or she clearly preferred the dark.

"It said to go to the back garden and take the path," I reminded her. "Keep walking."

A sudden crack of lighting lit the night sky, followed quickly by a clap of thunder.

"What was that?" Taylor gasped, grasping my cast.

"Thunder," I replied automatically.

She rolled her eyes. "Not that, *that.*"

She pointed a quaking finger at the house and I saw something move. A curtain fell back into place. My heart slammed against my ribs. Another crack of lightning and a face was illuminated at the next window. A pale, staring, panicked face.

"Oh my God," I said.

"What?" Noelle snapped, doubling back.

"I think I just saw Sawyer," I hissed. But when I looked back at the house, there was no one there.

"Sawyer? Where?" Ivy asked.

"At the third window on the second floor," I said tremulously, pointing.

"Maybe he's MT," Ivy suggested.

"But what would he be doing here?" I asked. "He didn't even know Cheyenne."

But he did know Ariana, I thought, pressing my lips together to keep from saying it out loud. They had both been on those trips to St. Barths for all those years. Had she kidnapped Sawyer and brought him here for some reason? To keep him from warning me? Or had she somehow roped him in to her sick plan, whatever it was?

"You were probably just seeing things," Noelle said with a sniff. "Come on. We have to get inside before we all die of exposure."

I was pretty sure it took a lot longer than fifteen minutes to die of exposure, especially on a relatively warm night, but I kept the thought to myself. I wasn't about to go back to the car by myself, and besides, everyone else was marching ahead. I cast one last look at the now-empty window and tried to clear my mind.

We crept around the back of the house until we found a lush but rain-flattened garden, all the roses and tulips and hydrangeas bowed toward the earth under the relentless torrent. The pebbled path led right past the back wall of the house and terminated at a set of double glass doors.

"What now?" Noelle asked.

On cue, my phone beeped. Kiran squealed and Taylor jumped. I tugged it from my pocket and read.

GO INSIDE THRU PARLOR & UPSTAIRS.

"Can I just say again that I don't like this?" Kiran whimpered.

Noelle grunted and reached for the door. She had to shove it hard to unstick it, but it opened. I held my breath as I followed her tentative steps inside. The room was an enclosed patio, filled with furniture covered by drop cloths. Noelle moved straight ahead, feeling her way in the dark and with the help of the occasional lightning flashes. The house was dead quiet, except for the sound of our tiptoed footsteps and the slamming beat of my pulse.

We came to the foot of a set of carpeted stairs. My phone beeped again. Kiran squealed.

"Stop doing that!" I hissed.

"I'm sorry! I can't help it!" she replied, hand at the base of her throat.

I read the text.

WHEN U GET 2 TOP, MAKE RT & GO 2 RM @ END OF HALL.

"Why doesn't he just come down?" Taylor asked, her voice trembling as she kneaded her wet fingers together. "What's with the cloak and dagger?"

"Clearly, MT likes to play," Ivy said, grabbing the bannister and starting up the stairs. Was it just me, or did it seem like she was enjoying this? I made a mental note to find her a good therapist later. As long as we all survived.

"You ready for this?" Noelle asked.

"I hope so," I replied.

I took her hand as we followed after Ivy and I was grateful when she didn't shrug me off. With every step, my heart rate seemed to speed up, my pulse pounding so loud in my ears I couldn't hear a thing. As my foot hit the top stair, I lost my balance and tipped sideways. As the door at the end of the hallway loomed ahead of us, every fiber of my being told me to run. Every instinct said this was wrong. But it was like I couldn't turn back. We were on a roller coaster, cresting the top of the hill, and all there was to do was plummet toward the earth, scream our heads off, and trust we'd arrive alive.

We paused outside the door.

"What do we do?" Taylor whispered.

"Well." Noelle released me and wiped her hands on the front of her wet jacket. "I'm going to open it."

She looked to me for confirmation, and I nodded. What else could I do?

Noelle slowly reached for the door. Her fingers trembled. She grazed the handle. And then my phone beeped.

"What now?" Ivy hissed.

I looked down at my phone, but the text was not from MT. It was from Sawyer's cell phone, and the message knocked all the wind out of me.

GET OUT NOW! RUN!!!!!

"Omigod," I gasped. "Run!"

We all turned around as one and froze. The overhead lights flickered on. My knees went out from under me and I grabbed Noelle to keep from going down. Standing right in front of us, not ten feet away, was Graham Hathaway, dry and clean and holding a gun trained right at my heart. But it wasn't him that stopped me cold. It was the person standing next to him, a menacing smirk on her pretty, familiar face.

"Cheyenne?" Ivy blurted.

"What's up, girls?" she asked in a perky voice.

Her cheeks were rosy, the smattering of freckles across her nose brought out by the glow of the lights. Her long blond hair was back in a black velvet headband, and she wore tan riding pants, a tight black

T-shirt, and black riding boots, like she'd just come in from exercising her horse.

"You're supposed to be dead," I croaked.

"Well, that's the thing I love about life, Reed," she replied, taking a few steps toward me. "It's just *full* of little surprises."

CRAZY BITCH

"No," I blurted, backing up. My mind was reeling so fast it made my eyes water, while my heart felt like it was being torn from my body, oh so slowly. "No, no, no! You're dead. I saw your dead body. I *held* your dead body!"

Cheyenne smirked as Graham advanced slightly, keeping me in his sights. If I wasn't so completely thrown by the presence of a living, breathing Cheyenne Martin, I'm sure I would have been freaking out over the fact that he had a gun trained on my chest. Unfortunately, for the moment, the walking-dead thing was a bit distracting.

"Amazing what modern science can do," Cheyenne said, shifting her weight from one foot to the other. Her gaze flicked over my friends dismissively. "I thought I told you to leave your friends in the car. Five murders are so much messier than one."

Kiran whimpered and clung to Noelle as her knees gave out from under her. My eyes flicked to Graham, who darted an uncertain look

over his shoulder at Cheyenne. I got the sudden hopeful feeling
that this was the first time she'd floated the idea of actual murder.
Whatever the case may be, he didn't seem quite so certain all of a
sudden.

I had backed my way behind Kiran and my eyes flicked to the heavy
pocket of her black hooded jacket. As she was currently cowering with
her eyes closed, I had a feeling I couldn't trust her to whip out that
stun gun at the appropriate moment. Surreptitiously, I reached into
her pocket, withdrew the gun, and slipped it inside the waistband of
my tight, soaking, itchy jeans.

"Graham, the door," Cheyenne said.

Keeping the gun aloft with one hand, Graham walked behind us
and opened the door. I wondered, briefly, if Sawyer was in there.

"Get inside," Cheyenne ordered, taking a few steps forward.
"Now!"

Taylor jumped and Kiran whimpered. Noelle and I turned and
walked through the door, helping Kiran along. Taylor was right behind
us, and Ivy brought up the rear.

"I don't want to die, Noelle," Kiran murmured. "I don't want
to die."

"Shhhhh. We'll get out of this," Noelle promised her. "Don't
worry."

We found ourselves inside an airy, high-ceilinged, dark-paneled
room. In the center was the biggest bed I'd ever seen, surrounded by
four posts and covered with swaths and swaths of pink fabrics and
lace. There were at least two dozen silk and satin pillows perfectly

arranged at the head of the bed, and a huge, swirling pink *C* embroidered into the bedspread.

"I can't believe you're doing this," Ivy said, backing her way into the room so she could face Cheyenne. "This isn't you."

"Yeah, well, a lot can happen to a person in a year. I, for instance, killed myself," Cheyenne said snarkily.

She let out an evil, barking laugh that sent chills down my spine. That was not Cheyenne's laugh. I had never liked the girl, but she'd always been a normal kind of obnoxious. This? This was off.

"Yeah, would you mind explaining that?" Ivy asked as Cheyenne closed the heavy oak door with a thud. "The whole school went to your funeral."

I kept a watchful eye on Graham as Ivy and Cheyenne talked. He walked over to the window and used the gun to move aside the curtain, peeking out. Then he slipped a cell phone from his pocket and checked it for messages. Where was his brother? Was he keeping him locked up here somewhere? I racked my brain, trying to place the room we were in now and figure out how far we were from the room in which I'd seen Sawyer, but my panicked mind was drawing a blank.

"Yes, but no one ever saw my body, right?" Cheyenne said, crossing her arms over her chest. "At least not after that first morning." Her eyes flicked to me, an amused glint shining from their depths. Suddenly I wondered if she'd heard what I'd said that morning when we'd found her unconscious on the floor of her room. Had I been emotional? Stupid? Scared? I couldn't recall much aside from the sight of her pale skin, the burst blood vessels around her eyes, and

Rose sobbing in the corner. Just remembering how devastated and scared and crushed my friends had been brought the hot, sour taste of hatred into my mouth. "My mother had to pay off a lot of people to make it look real, but it wasn't all that difficult. As soon as she found out who that Sabine girl really was, she knew she could blackmail her into doing anything in return for keeping quiet."

"You knew Sabine was Ariana's sister?" I demanded.

"Of course." Cheyenne lifted a shoulder. "What, are you miffed I didn't warn you? Why would I? My mother and I both wanted you dead. It would've been so much easier if the little twit had been able to pull it off."

"Yeah, but I was shot instead," Ivy snapped, her face burning red. "So that didn't go exactly as planned, did it?"

Cheyenne *tsk*ed under her breath. "I'm sorry about that, I," she said, pouting her lips. "Sometimes collateral damage is a necessary evil."

Ivy advanced on Cheyenne like she was going to tear her hair out, but Graham lifted the gun and aimed.

"Freeze!" he blurted, and Ivy did.

"Back up there with your friends," he said, waving the gun toward the rest of us. Taylor started to cry quietly and Kiran let out a low moan. Ivy took a couple of steps back.

"Sabine's mom is some kind of voodoo specialist or something," Cheyenne continued. "We told her we wanted to make it appear that I was dead, so she whipped up this awful sludge for me to drink, and voilà." She lifted her hands at her sides. "No more Cheyenne. Then it was just a matter of paying off Mrs. Naylor to confirm I was door-nailed and make a fake phone call to nine-one-one, and hiring some dudes to come in, throw a sheet over me, and cart me out of there. Two hours later I woke up back here with a massive headache, but otherwise alive and well."

"Why?" Noelle demanded, holding Kiran's hand at her side. "Why would you do that?"

"Yeah, if you wanted to leave Easton so badly, why not just leave?" I added.

Cheyenne's scowl turned venomous as she looked at me. "Because it was the only way we could be certain that I would be safe from *you*."

A chill went through me and my fingers twitched, curling inward. "Me? What did I ever do to you?"

"As long as you, a descendant of both Theresa Billings and Eliza Williams, are alive and well, none of the Billings Girls are safe."

"Not this again," Noelle groused, rolling her eyes. "Did you and your mom both drink from the same cup of crazy juice or what?"

"We're not crazy!" Cheyenne snapped, whirling on Noelle. "The curse is real. But it ends here. Tonight."

She straightened up and walked over to me, facing me toe-to-toe. Graham moved slowly behind me and suddenly I felt the cold steel end of the gun's barrel pressing against the back of my head. I tried to stare Cheyenne down, but all I saw were terrifying black and purple spots swirling across my vision.

"Tonight, Reed Brennan, you are finally, finally, *finally* going to die."

"Oh my God," Noelle said with a laugh. "I take it back. You're even *crazier* than your crazy bitch of a mom."

I knew what she was trying to do. She was trying to distract Cheyenne. Trying to give me a chance to escape. And for a moment, it worked. Cheyenne let out a guttural wail, turned toward Noelle, and brought her fist down and across Noelle's cheek and jawline so hard I heard the crack. Just like that, Noelle and Kiran both hit the floor. I let out an involuntary scream and Taylor started to cry in earnest. Kiran managed to push herself to her knees and weepily tried to revive Noelle, but my best friend, my sister, was out cold.

Now my heart began to pump furiously. Cheyenne had taken out Noelle? She was stronger than I could have imagined. My hand reached behind me for the stun gun, but it was too late. Cheyenne had already returned her attention to me. I dropped my hand at my side and lifted my chin, but it was all for show. I was suddenly certain that she was right. I was going to die here, tonight.

"One down," she said quietly. "Four to go."

Then Graham lifted the barrel of the gun away from my skull and brought it down so hard I saw stars—right before my knees hit the hardwood floor, and everything faded to black.

SAVING MYSELF

The incessant pounding in my skull brought me reluctantly back to consciousness. For a few long, painful moments I couldn't figure out where I was. Why were my arms wrenched behind me? Why were my knees throbbing? And what the hell was jabbing into the small of my back?

And then, suddenly, I remembered. The stun gun. The stun gun was still wedged into the waistband of my jeans. My eyes flew open, my heart surging with hope. I was in some kind of lounge room, complete with a wet bar, a circular leather couch facing a flat-screen TV, and a poker table surrounded by tall stools. The lights were on, but dim. My feet were bound as well as my hands, and my jacket—and therefore my cell phone—were gone. Luckily, I still had on my baggy black sweater, which accounted for the fact that Cheyenne and Graham hadn't found the stun gun while tying me up, which apparently one or both of them had done while I was knocked out. My friends were nowhere to be seen, and neither was evil walking-dead girl, but Graham was on the far side of the room, behind the bar, shoveling ice into a glass. Apparently he was going to need a tumbler full of cold vodka before shooting me in the head.

I wanted to say something to him, but then I realized I could use the fact that he still thought I was unconscious to my advantage. I looked around for a clock and found the glowing screen on the cable box. It was twelve minutes after twelve. If Josh kept his word, he'd be calling the police in exactly eighteen minutes. It had taken us about fifteen minutes to drive here. Which meant all I had to do was stall for half an hour or so and pray my friends were still alive.

Now if only I could think of a way to get my hands free. I tugged my wrists apart and found that the ties weren't exactly tight, probably because my cast had gotten in the way. If I could tear the twine even a little bit, I should be able to slip it off. Jagged barnacles had worked wonders back on that island paradise I was trapped on over Christmas break, but there didn't seem to be anything sharp lying around.

And then it hit me. Maybe I didn't need something sharp. Maybe I could singe the twine with the stun gun, fraying it until I was able to pull my wrists apart.

Slowly, quietly, I leaned forward, dragging the back hem of my sweater upward with my tied hands. I had just angled my wrists over the business end of the stun gun, which was sticking out of my waistband by a few inches, when three flaws in my plan suddenly occurred to me. First, the stun gun made that crackling noise, which would definitely catch Graham's attention. Second, if I attempted this, there was a solid chance I'd set my cast on fire. Third, there was also a solid chance I'd stun myself.

I glanced up at Graham as he poured brown liquid over the ice. The gun was on the edge of the bar. Screw it. Who cared if I stunned myself? This was the only plan I had, and if I didn't at least try, I was going to be dead. Which was a lot worse than shocked and twitching on the floor. And if I managed to set myself on fire, it would, at the very least, create a diversion.

I took a deep breath and coughed, pressing the small of my back against the wall as I leaned forward. The stun gun sizzled to life, my coughing covering the sound, and I didn't get a shock. I did, however, get a whiff of the faintest scent of fibers burning. I just hoped it was the twine and not the cast.

Graham dropped his glass, grabbed the gun, and started toward me. I tugged at my wrists, but they didn't give. Shit.

"You're awake," he said.

I kept coughing, kept pressing, shaking my head. The burning scent filled my nostrils. How long would it be until he caught a whiff?

"Water," I said. "I need water."

Graham glanced over his shoulder at the wet bar. My arms ached from the effort of not moving while my body was racked with fake coughs. Any second I was going to shock myself.

"Please, Graham," I choked. "Water."

He seemed to decide I wasn't much of a threat. As he turned and went back toward the bar, I yanked my hands apart as hard as I possibly could and they came free. The twine tumbled, singed, to the floor, just as Graham turned around again. My heart hit my throat. I kept my hands behind my back and shifted so that my butt came down atop the twine. I could feel the warm, burnt ends through the fabric of my jeans.

Slowly, Graham approached me with the water in one hand, the gun in the other. He crouched in front of me and held the glass to my lips, tipping it upward. The cold liquid filled my throat and actually did make me feel a bit better. I gauged my chances of knocking the gun out of his hand and getting to it before he did, all with my feet tied together and a cast on one arm.

Answer? Not good.

But at least my hands were free. That gave me the advantage of surprise. Hopefully I had a few minutes to figure out how to use it.

His nostrils flared and he glanced around. "Do you smell something burning?"

I lifted my shoulders. "Nope. And thanks."

Graham looked down at the half-empty glass of water and suddenly appeared to be offended by it—like it illustrated some kind of weakness. He got up and dropped it on a side table, out of my reach, sloshing some liquid over the rim.

"Don't know why I bothered. You're gonna be dead soon anyway," he said callously.

"Graham," I said, my stomach twisting into knots. "Why are you doing this? I get Cheyenne with the crazy, but why you? I thought we were friends."

"We could've been," he said, clenching his jaw. "If it wasn't for *him*."

The word "him" was laced with venom.

"Josh? This is about Josh again?" I demanded.

His eyes widened incredulously. "He killed my sister!"

"He did *not* kill her!" I blurted, my heart pounding over my own recklessness. I couldn't believe I was going to die for the two most obscure, insane reasons anyone could imagine dying for—some hundred-year-old supposed curse and the fact that a girl I never knew had dated my boyfriend two years ago, then taken her own life. "Jen killed herself. I'm sorry to put it so bluntly, but it's the truth! You're going to kill me because Jen committed suicide? Do you not realize how crazy that is?"

Graham's mouth flattened into an angry line and I saw his jaw working, tightening and releasing, tightening and releasing. "You sound just like Sawyer," he griped.

Sawyer. Sawyer was here somewhere. He wasn't planning on hurting his own brother too, was he?

"Where is Sawyer, Graham?" I asked, trying to keep my voice even as I looked at the clock. It was now 12:20. "Is he okay?"

"Of course he's okay," Graham said with a scoff. "What do you think I'm gonna do, kill my own brother?"

He brought his hand, the one holding the gun, to his heart and pounded. Tears filled his eyes and I took a deep breath. He was becoming unhinged, and unhinged was not going to be good for me.

"I took that stupid phone he was using to warn you and we locked him here in one of the bedrooms until we could be done with this," Graham said. "That's how I got you here tonight. I texted you the directions from his dummy phone."

So it was Sawyer all along. Sawyer was MT. Of course. It all made sense. He couldn't come to me and tell me what was going on, or go to the police, without implicating Graham, so instead he'd tried to protect me anonymously—to protect us both. And what had he gotten for his efforts? He'd ended up jailed by his own brother and crazy Cheyenne.

"I just don't get why he doesn't get it," Graham rambled, pacing away from me, his heavy shoes clomping across the gleaming wood floor. The second his back was turned I withdrew my hands from behind my back and yanked at the knot around my legs. But seconds later he started to turn around again and I had to hide my fingers after getting exactly nowhere. I bit my lip in frustration and tried not to let my desperation show in my eyes. "Josh Hollis drove Jen to kill herself. She was perfectly fine before he broke her heart. If it wasn't for him, she'd still be alive right now!"

"I know you believe that, Graham, but please, think about it," I said. "People in their right mind don't kill themselves over breakups. They get makeovers, they find rebound guys, they post nasty videos about the guy on YouTube. Something had to be fundamentally wrong with her if she was going to—"

"There was nothing wrong with Jen!" he screeched, storming toward me across the floorboards creaking beneath his feet. "She was my best friend! I loved her more than I loved anyone else in the world. And Josh Hollis took her away from me. So that's why I'm going to take you away from him."

He pointed the gun at my head and cocked it. My heart stopped beating. His hand shook and his eyes welled. At any moment that thing could go off. At any moment my brains could be splattered all over the wall behind me. If there was ever a time to make a move, it was now.

"Think about Sawyer, Graham. If you kill me, he'll never forgive you," I said, trying to keep my voice steady. "And then you'll have lost your brother *and* your sister."

"Shut up!" he said, bending and straightening his elbow, bringing the gun even closer to my skull. I wanted to reach out and grab it, but what if doing that made it go off? What if one flinch caused him to pull the trigger?

"You're better than this, Graham," I said, frantically rubbing my ankles together to try to free them from the twine. "Think about your father. Think about your brother. Think about your girlfriend."

I tasted bile as I thought about Missy. Thought about how happy she would be once she heard I was gone.

Graham's eyes narrowed. "You know, maybe I'll just end you right now."

At that moment the door opened. I prayed it was the police, but then I saw the shiny black boots in the doorway.

"Graham! You promised you wouldn't do it without me!" Cheyenne whined.

Graham lowered the gun and started to turn. I used the moment of distraction to grab the stun gun out of my waistband with my right hand. Cheyenne's eyes went wide, but she was too late. I lunged for Graham and hit the button, shocking him right in the lower leg. He went down, hard, and the gun went off. The shot was so loud my ears instantly began to ring. For a second the whole world went black as fear overtook every inch of my body, but then I realized I wasn't hit.

And Cheyenne was on the floor.

"You bitch!" she screeched, holding on to her shin. Blood seeped between her fingers even as she tried to shimmy on her side toward the gun. My legs still bound, I crawled toward the gun on my one good hand and my knees, snaking past a twitching Graham Hathaway. Cheyenne reached out one blood-covered hand, just as my own fingers clasped around the gun's handle. I trained it right on her face and braced my cast against the back of the couch, struggling my way to my feet.

"Don't. Move," I said through my teeth.

Cheyenne gaped at me for a moment, like she couldn't believe I was standing there alive. Like she couldn't believe she had lost. Then she curled into a ball and started to cry.

At that moment Sawyer and Noelle came bursting into the room, out of breath but very much alive, with half a dozen cops at their backs. I looked at them as they took in the scene: Graham on his back, drooling out the side of his mouth; Cheyenne mewling and bleeding all over the floor; and me clutching a gun I had no clue how to use, precariously leaned against the back of the couch with my ankles tied together.

"Thanks, guys," I said. "But this time I saved myself."

CRAZY PEOPLE

"Every time something like this happens to you, I think there's no way anything like this can possibly happen to you again, because what are the chances?" Noelle said, leaning against a stone planter at the front of Cheyenne's house as the evil walking-dead girl herself was loaded into an ambulance. "But then—"

"It always happens again," I finished for her.

She nodded, narrowing her eyes. "Have you ever thought about getting a gun? You looked pretty badass back there, holding that thing over Cheyenne. And if anyone I knew ever needed one . . ."

I mentally scrolled through all my near-death experiences: Ariana on the Billings roof; Sabine at Kiran's birthday party; pretty much all of St. Barths; and now this. "I'm anti guns, but you do make an interesting point," I conceded.

Noelle lifted an arm and laid it around my shoulder, pulling me to her side. "We have met more than our fair share of bat-shit crazy people over the past two years, haven't we?"

We both watched as a pair of uniformed police officers dragged Graham past us, his hands cuffed behind him, and practically tossed him into a police car. My heart felt sick and heavy and withered, like it was being bathed in battery acid. Graham Hathaway. I never would have thought he had it in him.

"Yes," I replied, holding my cast against my chest and pushing my other hand into the pocket of my jacket, which had been returned to me by Detective Hauer. He was now standing about thirty yards away, taking statements from Taylor, Kiran, and Ivy. I had already called Josh to thank him for phoning in my backup, but he'd said that when he'd called, the police were already on their way. Apparently, Sawyer had dialed 911 right after texting me to run. I guess his phone call had been more convincing than mine. In any case I was practically itching to get home to Josh for a nice, long hug. "Yes, we have."

"Do you think it'll be better at Yale?" Noelle pondered, tipping her face up toward the now clearing sky.

"God, it better be," I replied.

And somehow, we both managed to laugh.

A familiar figure appeared at the door of the house. Sawyer. He locked eyes with me and I could feel all the sorrow and fear pouring off of him. I stood up straight as he approached, his steps tentative, like if I made any sudden movements he was ready to bolt. I tried to smile. Sawyer, of all people, had nothing to fear from me.

"Hey," he said.

"Hey."

Noelle looked back and forth between the two of us and tugged out her phone. "I think I'm gonna call Dash."

Then she moved a few feet away, giving us room to talk.

"I am so, *so* sorry, Reed," Sawyer began, reaching toward me, but then letting his hand fall, like he didn't know what to do with it. "I knew Graham was trying to sabotage Billings, but I had no clue he was going to try to hurt you, I swear."

"I know," I said.

"You do?" Sawyer asked, dubious.

"Sawyer, I know you. If you knew he was going to hurt me, you would have told someone," I said, walking up a couple of steps to sit down on a flat portion of the wide stair wall. The rain had stopped, but the concrete was cold and still wet. I thought about moving, but decided I was too exhausted to care.

"I only just figured it out last night. I walked in on him Skyping with Cheyenne, talking about him stealing my father's gun," Sawyer said, sitting next to me, his shoulders hunched. "When I confronted him about it, he said it was all a joke and then he kind of tricked me into coming here. I was able to send you that one text about not going to the banquet tonight before they locked me up and took my phones. I managed to lift mine off of him when he came in to check on me just before you guys got here. That's how I sent that warning text and called the police. I'm just sorry it took so long."

I nodded, trying to process everything. "So with the Billings stuff, you were trying to help me, but still protect your brother."

"Yeah. I'm such an idiot." He looked over as the sirens whooped to life and the ambulance carrying Cheyenne zoomed off, followed by two police cars. "Like he needed so much protecting."

His eyes filled with tears and his bottom lip quivered. I put my arm around him and squeezed, my heart filling and swelling and breaking for him. First he'd lost his mother, then his sister, and now Graham. I couldn't imagine what this was doing to him.

"Sawyer?"

We both flinched, and I let go of him. Mr. Hathaway jogged toward us, his tan trench coat billowing out behind him, a haggard look on his face. I saw his car idling at the curb as he swooped in on Sawyer and wrapped him up in a hug.

"What happened, son?" he asked. "What happened?"

Sawyer just started to bawl. He cried all over his father's sweater, clutching on to him for dear life. I stood up slowly as his dad whispered into his hair. Now it was my turn to tactfully walk away. A few yards off, Graham stared out from the back window of the police car—staring at the family he'd destroyed. Can't say I didn't warn him.

At the bottom of the steps, Ivy, Taylor, Kiran, and Noelle had all gathered. I joined them slowly, feeling more broken and tired with each step.

"So," Noelle said.

"So," Ivy echoed.

"Detective Hauer told us they arrested Daniel Ryan at the airport," Taylor said. "He was the one who tried to kidnap you tonight, and the second he realized Trey might have seen his car, he bolted."

"Okay, I don't know who has the more effed-up DNA, the Kane-Martins or the Ryans," Kiran said, splaying her fingers.

"It's a toss-up," I replied.

"Do you think we could maybe get together one time without any cops involved?" Taylor asked.

I snorted a laugh, but it was a short-lived one. "There's still one thing I don't get. How did Graham get hooked up with Cheyenne in the first place?"

"My money's on Paige," Noelle replied instantly, shaking her still drying hair back from her face. "We already know she was buddy-buddy with the alums who tried to kill you guys on your birthday, so clearly she bought into all that curse crap too. She's probably known all this time that Cheyenne was alive, and when Cheyenne decided she wanted to come after you, she needed eyes at Easton—"

"And Paige knows all about Josh and Jen's history, so it wasn't the biggest leap to make, thinking Graham would help her," Taylor finished.

"In a disgusting, twisted way, that actually makes sense," Ivy said, shaking her head.

"Holy crap. Ivy Slade just agreed with me," Noelle said jokingly. "Does anyone have a pen so we can write this down? I need witnesses."

Ivy rolled her eyes and shoved her hands into her pockets, drawing her jacket closer against a cool breeze. "Well, we already know Paige tried to kill Reed. I'll bet when it didn't work and she got locked up, Cheyenne convinced Daniel to do it, and when that didn't work out, she moved on to Graham."

"Notice how she never had a plan that involved getting actual blood on her own hands," Noelle said flatly.

"Are you kidding?" Kiran blurted. "Blood is *far* too messy for Cheyenne Martin."

"Well, she ended up covered in it anyway," I said, staring off after the ambulance. "It just turned out it was her own."

We took a collective deep breath and I turned to look up at the castlelike home Cheyenne had apparently spent the past few months locked up inside. I couldn't help remembering what it had looked like the night of our off-campus Christmas party last year. All the windows aglow with light, happy revelers waving around champagne glasses, a dozen overprivileged and life-clueless kids hanging out in the hot tub. That night I had felt truly included for the first time— like a real Billings Girl. I had thought that Noelle, Kiran, Taylor, and Ariana would be my best friends forever.

Until about an hour after we left, when Ariana tried to kill me.

"It's so weird," Taylor mused as if reading my mind. "The last time we were here, we were all together . . . even Ariana. We had no idea how insane things were about to get."

"Oh, things got weird way before then," I said, looking down at my feet as I cradled my cast with my other hand. I scuffed my sneaker against the edge of the stone step. "They got weird the second I stepped on the Easton campus."

Noelle made a disbelieving sound in the back of her throat. "Don't tell me you're starting to believe the propaganda," she said. Suddenly, an overwhelmingly heavy sadness threatening to drag me under. "You are, aren't you? You think you really are cursed."

My friends exchanged incredulous looks as my eyes stung and blurred. "I don't know. Sometimes I just feel really, really unlucky."

"Unlucky?" Ivy said incredulously. "Do you realize how many times you've cheated death this week alone?" She blew out her lips and shook her head. "From where I'm standing, you're the luckiest bitch on Earth."

We all just stood there for a moment, until a bubble of laughter escaped from my mouth and we all started to giggle.

"Since when are you a glass-half-full kind of girl?" I asked.

Ivy lifted her shoulders. "Things change."

"Man, do they ever," Kiran said, slinging her arm over my shoulder as Mr. Hathaway and Sawyer walked by, huddled together, and approached Detective Hauer. "I used to think Graham was hot."

I laughed, turned toward Kiran, and hugged her, then felt Noelle's arms go around my back. Soon Taylor and even Ivy had joined in on the group hug—one big mess of tangled hair, designer perfume, and chilled skin. I ducked my head inside the cocoon my friends had formed for me and smiled.

Maybe I wasn't so unlucky after all.

GOOD SURPRISE

"This is definitely one of the best ideas you've ever had," I told Josh a week later, cuddling back into his arms under the shade of our favorite oak tree at the center of the Easton Academy campus. I tore off a bit of the croissant I was holding and reached it up over my shoulder. He opened his mouth and snatched it from my fingers with his teeth.

"Agreed."

Laid out in front of us was an old-fashioned picnic basket, overflowing with more croissants, fruit salad, one thermos of orange juice, and another of coffee. It was the morning of graduation, and all across the sunlit campus seniors strolled with their parents in suits and dresses, taking pictures in front of dorms and pointing out places of interest. There was this odd sense of finality in the air, mixed with the overwhelming, airy feeling of new beginnings. Flowers bloomed along the stone walks and bees buzzed from bud to bud. Birds chirped merrily overhead as a warm breeze tickled my bare arms. As much as I knew I would miss having Josh here with me next year, I couldn't help feeling happy, hopeful. I didn't want that feeling to ever end.

"I have a surprise for you," Josh said, shifting his weight behind me. I turned my head to look up at him.

"Yeah?"

He extricated a piece of folded paper from his back pocket and handed it to me. I traded my croissant for the heavy paper stock, my pulse giving a little thrill. I had a feeling I knew what this was, and as soon as I unfolded the page, my hopes were confirmed.

Dear Mr. Hollis,

Welcome to Cornell University! We are pleased to inform you that you have been accepted off the wait list and we have reserved a space for you in this fall's freshman class.

"You did it!" I cried, throwing my arms up. My cast caught his chin with a crack.

"Ow!"

"Oh God. Sorry!" I circled my arms around him anyway and kissed the spot I'd bruised. "I'm so happy for you!"

"I know, but you don't have to beat me up over it," Josh joked, hugging me back. He buried his face in my shoulder and kissed the tip of my collarbone. "I couldn't have done it without you."

"Actually, you probably would have gotten in the first time if not for me," I said pragmatically.

Josh pondered this, then clutched the back of my hair with one hand. "Possibly. But life would have been a lot less interesting."

We both smiled and he leaned in to kiss me. I touched my fingertips to his face as we moved in to each other, savoring each and every last touch and sigh and breath. Everything felt crisper this morning. More real. More significant. I suppose that's how everything feels at ends and beginnings.

Then someone cleared his throat nearby. Seriously nearby. Josh and I both looked up. Headmaster Hathaway glowered down at us. His skin looked almost gray, and his normally coiffed hair had a scraggly look about it. It was the first time I'd laid eyes on the man in a week, and Sawyer had been absent from campus all that time as well.

"Pardon me for interrupting."

"Headmaster Hathaway," I said, because I couldn't think of anything else to say, couldn't imagine what he wanted.

"I came over here to say I'm sorry. For what happened with Graham." He lifted his eyes and looked out across campus toward the Billings construction site. "I had no idea he was so troubled."

"What's going to happen to him?" I asked.

"We're not sure yet," he replied. "Possibly jail time, definitely treatment . . . it's too soon to say."

"I'm so sorry, sir," Josh offered. "For everything that's happened to your—"

The depth of pain that flashed through the headmaster's eyes as he looked at Josh stopped my breath. I put my hand on Josh's arm and he stopped talking. Clearly, talking to Josh reminded the

headmaster of Jen, and that was the last thing he needed to be dwell-
ing on right now.

"We just both really hope that things get better for you," I said,
hoping it didn't sound trite. "You and Sawyer . . . *and* Graham."

"Thank you. Considering the circumstances, that's very kind of
you," the headmaster said. "Obviously we won't be back here next
year." He cleared his throat and turned to face me fully. "I wish you
luck, Miss Brennan. With all your . . . endeavors."

In the background we all heard a crash, and the headmaster
flinched. I held my breath, but no shouts or screams came. Apparently
it was a run-of-the-mill construction noise, nothing more.

"Thank you," I told the headmaster.

"Well, then." He tried for a smile, but it came out as a grim frown.
"Have a good day."

Then he turned on his heel and speed-walked away. I wondered if
he was going to attend the graduation ceremony that afternoon. From
the looks of it, probably not. He was practically leaving a fire track
behind him as he hoofed it for Hull Hall. I was sure he couldn't get out
of here fast enough.

"Is it just me, or have we gone through a lot of headmasters?" I
said, trying for levity as I leaned back into Josh's waiting arms again.

"Three in two years? Yeah, that's not normal," Josh agreed, handing my croissant back to me.

"I wonder who it'll be next year," I said, taking a small bite. "If
tradition holds, it'll be someone who's offended by my very existence
and will do everything in their power to make my life miserable."

"Nah," Josh said with a smirk. "Fourth time's the charm."

I laughed and followed the headmaster with my eyes until he had disappeared inside Hull Hall. If he wasn't coming back next year, that meant Sawyer wouldn't be here either. I felt a pang of loss deep inside my chest and let out a sigh. So many people had come and gone out of my life lately. . . . It was getting old. But it also reminded me of who was truly important.

I tilted my head up and looked Josh in the eye.

"What?" he asked quietly.

"Nothing. I just love you," I said.

Josh smiled and softly kissed my lips. "I love you, too."

ALL YOU

"Tiffany Roxanna Goulbourne!"

I cheered as Tiffany strolled across the stage in her dark blue graduation gown. While most students had a few cameras trained on them as they accepted their diplomas, Tiffany lifted her camera out from the inside of her bell sleeve, held it above her head, and snapped off a few shots of her own as Dean Marshall attempted to hand her the scroll. Everyone cheered as Tiffany shook the dean's hand and accepted her diploma, moving her gold tassel from one side of her cap to the other as she descended the stairs on the far side of the stage.

"I can't believe they're actually graduating," Constance said, lifting a tissue to her nose in the chair next to mine.

"I can't believe they got such a bloody gorgeous day," Astrid added, squinting up at the sun from behind her thick sunglasses. "You know that when we graduate it'll be the rainstorm to end all rainstorms."

"No negativity today," I admonished. "It's going to be beautiful. Even better than this."

My friends all eyed me, surprised, but I ignored them.

"Shh! Josh is next!"

"Joshua Matthew Hollis!"

Josh strolled up to stage, looking confident and handsome and happy. His parents and brothers and sisters were a cheering section unto themselves on the other side of the aisle, giving him a standing ovation. I stood up too, clapping as best I could with my cast, and smiled at Josh's brother Lynn across the way. Josh shook the dean's hand, took his diploma, and held it in his fist above his head. I laughed, my chest welling up with pride and happiness and sadness all at once. He found my eyes as he walked off stage and I blew him a kiss before sitting down again.

"I just can't believe I'm not going to be a freshman anymore," Amberly said, touching up her berry-colored lip gloss. "Is it just me, or has this has been the longest year ever?"

"It's not you," I agreed.

"It's going to be so weird around here without them, isn't it?" Lorna said, leaning forward at the far end of the aisle. "Portia, the Twin Cities, and everyone?"

"Weird, or just really, really awesome," Kiki put in, snapping her gum.

I looked up and down the line at the five of them—Constance with her red hair back in a bun, her white-and-pink striped shirt buttoned and pressed; Astrid in her black boatneck T-shirt with about a hundred silver chains around her neck and her boots spattered with paint; Kiki, growing out her short blond hair so that it now stuck out from behind her ears as if she'd had an electric shock, wearing a floral baby-doll dress no one else on campus could pull off; Lorna in a dark pink shift dress, beaded necklace, and straightened black hair. I had even cleared a special place in my heart for matchy-matchy Amberly in her blue-and-white striped boatneck tee, wide-legged white pants, and blue slingbacks. Next year, we were the returning Billings Girls. Next year, we would set the tone.

"I'm thinking awesome," I said.

Then a movement on the other side of campus caught my eye. The doors of Pemberly were thrown open and two uniformed police officers dragged Missy Thurber out, her hands cuffed behind her back. Most of the crowd didn't notice, as their backs were to the dorms, but my friends and I saw.

"What the hell?" I whispered.

"I heard she knew all about Cheyenne and Graham's plans," Constance whispered, so quietly I almost couldn't hear.

"I'll bet they're arresting her as an accessory," Kiki put in.

The police quickly and discreetly hauled Missy around a corner and out of sight, before all the influential alumni and proud parents could catch a glimpse. I thought it would feel satisfying, having my oldest and most annoying nemesis finally expunged from campus, but I just felt hollow. Was that it? Were my enemies finally and truly all gone?

"Are you all right, Reed?" Amberly asked as we all faced forward again.

I nodded, blinking in the sunlight. "I'll be fine."

"Noelle Theresa Lange!"

All six of us jumped to our feet to cheer for Noelle, and I did my best to applaud the negative feelings away. On the other side of the aisle, Dash and his family stood up as well, along with Noelle's mother and grandmother. A lump of sorrow gathered in my throat, realizing it must have been killing Noelle that her father wasn't here to see this. Tears gathered in my eyes as I applauded, but Noelle showed no such emotion. She walked right up to the dean, her chin up, her dark hair loose down her back, her gold and white valedictorian tassels hanging over her shoulders. When the Easton photographer was ready, she clasped the dean's hand, took her diploma, and smiled her perfect, winning smile into the lens. Then she turned toward her family and Dash, then toward me. The look in her eye was half amusement, half pride. And then she walked off stage.

Two seconds later, my phone beeped. For a split second I thought it might be another menacing message, another warning, another confusion, but when I whipped out my phone, the text was from Noelle.

IT'S ALL YOU, GLASS-LICKER. DON'T SCREW IT UP.

I covered my mouth with my hand. Classic Noelle.

Just like that, it was over. The end of Noelle Lange's era at Easton. As I sat down again, I didn't know whether to laugh or cry.

So I did a little bit of both.

PAST, PRESENT, FUTURE

"I can't believe Gage's parents own this place!" I shouted to Ivy, trying to make myself heard over the music. Kiran, Taylor, and Natasha Crenshaw all danced in our small circle at the center of the dance floor as well, and every time one of us spoke, we all smiled and nodded, but I hadn't heard a word anyone said all night and I was sure they hadn't either.

Ivy leaned in toward me, resting her hands on my shoulders as we danced and leaning toward my ear. "I know! They have seaside resorts all over the country!"

"And one day it'll all be mine!" Gage announced, appearing at our sides with two bottles of champagne clutched in each hand, his fingers woven around their necks. He spread his arms wide, his linen jacket opening to reveal the tight white T-shirt underneath.

Ivy rolled her eyes as he slung one arm around her shoulder under the huge, crystal chandelier. "I got two for you and two for me.

Whaddaya say we go up to my personal suite and have a chug contest?"

Shoving him away with both hands, Ivy shook her head. "We practically just got here!"

He winked at her. "I'll be back in an hour then."

With that he plunged into the crowd, kissing a few cheeks and hugging it out with some guys as he went, clearly in his element. Suddenly a pair of slim arms encircled my neck from behind.

"Hey, Tiff," I said as she rested her chin on my shoulder. "What's up?"

"We're going outside for a breather," she said, tilting her head toward a crowd of Billings Girls behind her. "Wanna join?"

I glanced at Ivy and she nodded, out of breath. "We're in."

Together we wove our way through the dancing throng on the marble floor, eventually coming to the huge French doors, which opened up onto a wide, wooden plank deck overlooking the ocean. We all tottered in our heels over to the stone railing, laughing and trying to catch our breath. Down below, more Easton students milled on the beach, hanging out on the cushy lounge chairs set up to face the water. The ocean crashed, and out near the horizon lights twinkled on the decks of distant boats.

"Champagne, ladies?" A handsome waiter in a light blue shirt and white pants paused nearby with a tray full of glasses.

"You know us *so* well," Vienna trilled, selecting one for her and one for London.

Rose and Portia giggled as we all took our own glasses. I looked around at the circle of my friends—Kiran, Taylor, Natasha, Ivy,

Tiffany, Rose, Portia, London, Vienna, Shelby, Constance, Lorna, Kiki, and Astrid—everyone dressed in their colorful cocktail gear, everyone smiling and glowing, and felt completely and utterly at peace. The only people missing were Noelle, who was off with Dash somewhere, and Amberly, who was a freshman and therefore not eligible to attend the party.

"Well?" Kiran said. "What should we toast to?"

Everyone looked at me. "How about—"

"Um, Reed?"

Everyone lowered their glasses as I turned away. Diana Waters and Shane Freundel, two junior classmates of mine, approached tentatively. Diana bit her lip and glanced over at Kiki, her former roommate and one of her best friends.

"Sorry to interrupt," she said, clutching her purse in both hands. "I just wanted to ask you before we all left for the summer . . . how do we apply to be in Billings next year?"

I smiled. Junior girls had been coming up to me all day asking me this same question, and every time someone did, I felt more and more like a rock star—and more certain I'd done the right thing by bringing Billings back. But now I felt the mood among my friends shift. Some of them were probably realizing, not for the first time, that they were out of here—and that they were bound to be replaced in Billings.

"Every rising junior and senior girl will receive an application sometime in the next month," I said. "As long as you get it in on time, you'll be considered."

"Cool. Thanks," Shane said.

She glanced around longingly at my friends. It was a look I knew well. I'd seen it on the faces of tons of girls over the past couple of years—people who wanted nothing more than to know what it was like to be a part of the Billings inner circle. I licked my lips, feeling guilty for excluding anyone, but now was not the time. They'd have their chance next year. For now, my senior friends deserved to get to celebrate with their sisters.

"Well. See ya," Diana said finally.

The two girls strolled off slowly, as if hoping to be stopped and invited back, but I resisted the urge and turned around again, re-forming the circle.

"It's so weird that we're not gonna be here next year," London mused, brushing her hair away from her face with her fingertips.

"Promise you won't let in anyone heinous, Reed," Shelby said, spreading her manicured fingers wide.

I laughed. "I promise to try."

"So are we gonna toast or what?" Portia asked.

I nodded and lifted my glass, looking around at Kiran, Taylor, and Natasha; at Ivy, Tiffany, and the other seniors; at Constance, Lorna, Kiki, and Astrid. "To all Billings Girls," I said, my voice almost cracking. "Past, present, and future."

"To the Billings Girls!" my friends shouted.

We all laughed as our glasses came together in the center of the circle, clinking against the starry sky.

GOING HOME

My bags were packed. My tickets booked. My car waiting at the curb in front of the dormitory circle. Junior year was over. I had somehow survived. It was time to go home.

But going back to Croton never really felt like going home. I felt more like I was going away on a two-month vacation and when I came back, my home would be here again. As much as I loved my mother, father, and brother, as much torture and insanity as I had endured at Billings over the past two years . . . the dorm had always felt more like home. It was where I'd made my first real friendships, where I'd lived when I first found love, where I'd started to figure out who I was and who I was going to become.

I stood behind the blue, swagged rope surrounding the Billings construction site, the sunlight glinting against my mirrored sunglasses. It was amazing how quickly the building was coming together. Already the entire five-story frame was in place, the steel and wood beams rising up toward the sky. On the top floor of that building would be my room—the room Constance and I had decided to share—with windows looking out across the quad and the rest of campus. I reached up and touched Eliza Williams's locket, imagining she was standing right next to me and smiling.

It was all going to be different next year. I could feel it in my bones, in my heart, in my soul. This Billings really would be a new Billings. Ariana was gone. Sabine was gone. Cheyenne was gone. Even Missy was gone. As I listened to the sounds of the saws buzzing, the hammers pounding, the gears on the machinery grinding, I felt as if Thomas was really and truly being put to rest. As if every last awful thing that had happened to me over the past two years was firmly behind me. There was no place to go but forward.

"Why so pensive, Glass-Licker?" Noelle asked, strolling up behind me.

She cradled two champagne glasses against her chest, and held a bottle in her free hand.

"Noelle!" I hissed, glancing around the quad. Several faculty members and students still milled about, waiting for their rides or saying their good-byes for the summer. "It's the middle of the day."

"So?" She handed me the bottle and held out the two glasses. "They can't do anything to me now. I'm outta here."

The bottle was cold in my hand. "What about me?" I said through my teeth.

Noelle scoffed, tilting her head back. "Please. You own this place now."

My cheeks turned pink with pleasure. She was, at least, partly right. I owned the dorm being erected right in front of us, and with the amount of money I'd either donated to or generated for Easton Academy over the past three months, I may as well have held the deed to the place.

I turned my back toward the quad and popped open the champagne. It overflowed, splashing foam near our feet, and we both jumped back, letting out little happy squeals. Noelle held out the glasses and I tipped the bottle over each in turn.

"To old friends and new beginnings," Noelle offered, holding her glass toward mine.

I lifted an eyebrow. "To you never, ever, *ever* calling me Glass-Licker ever again," I replied.

She lifted a mirrored eyebrow, considering. "Done."

We clinked glasses and sipped. I wondered how long that resolution would actually last.

"So. This is where you're going to be living next year," she mused, tilting her head as she looked up at the building's skeleton. "It's a tad bare."

I chuckled, then sighed, shaking my head as I looked down at the grass between our feet, my aged Converse lined up next to her shiny Jimmy Choos.

"Actually, I've given it some serious thought, and after everything that's happened over the past two years, I've decided something."

Noelle took a long sip of her champagne. "Really? What's that?"

I turned toward her, adopted my most grave expression, and looked her in the eye.

"From now on, I'm going to be homeschooled."

Noelle's jaw dropped. She almost fumbled her glass. "What? No! You can't. Reed, you can't possibly think that—"

Ever so slowly, my serious frown turned into a shit-eating grin. Noelle's eyes widened and she gasped.

"You bitch!"

"Gotcha!"

She slapped my arm with her free hand, shaking her head at me in wonder as she drained the dregs of her champagne.

"Nice one, Glass-Licker."

"Hey!"

"You deserved it! God! You really had me for a second there!"

We turned our steps toward the underclassman dorms and the circle beyond, where trunks snapped closed, hugs were thrown, car doors popped shut. Someone, somewhere, let out a scream, but it was a happy scream. The scream of a girl seeing someone she hadn't seen in a long time, or freaking out over summer plans. I gave Noelle a hug as the driver loaded my things into the back of the town car. I would be seeing her in a few weeks when Josh and I came to visit her in New York, but for now she was bound for the islands with Dash. Before getting in the car I took one last look up at the windows of Bradwell, the dorm that had been my very first home on campus—ever so briefly—and at Pemberly, where I'd spent the past few tumultuous months, then I sat down on the velvety seat, and the driver slammed the door.

"Need to make any stops on the way, miss?" the driver asked me as he turned onto the drive.

"No thanks," I replied. "Just to the airport."

"Can't wait to get home, eh?" he asked pleasantly.

I angled myself so I could see the stone facades of the Easton campus in the rearview mirror, watching the very top of the Billings frame until we dipped down the hill and it was out of sight.

"Yeah," I said giddily, imagining how it would look the next time I saw it—all covered in stone with the windows shining and the new cornerstone firmly in place. "I can't wait."

ACKNOWLEDGMENTS

It's hard to believe how long I've been working on Private. We're talking two moves, two babies, and a few bestsellers ago. So many editors, publishers, marketing experts, and agents have been instrumental in making this series as intriguing as it is, and as successful as it is, so I'm taking this opportunity to try to thank them all now. They are, in no particular order . . . Josh Bank, Lanie Davis, Emily Meehan, Sara Shandler, Les Morgenstein, Lynn Weingarten, Katie del Rosario, Kristin Marang, Courtney Bongiolatti, Julia Maguire, Justin Chanda, Paul Crichton, Lucille Rettino, and, of course, Sarah Burnes.

I also want to thank my friends and fellow authors for always supporting and recommending my work, especially Shira Citron, Sharren Bates, Wendy Stewart, Ally Stevenson, Jessica Freundel, Meredith and Jason Rothouse, Roxy Menhaji, Jeff Palkevich, Courtney Sheinmel, Elizabeth Scott, Gayle Forman, Sara Shepard, Susane Colasanti, Jenny Han, Jen Calonita, Julia DeVillers, Kay Cassidy, Micol Ostow, Stephanie

Hale, and David Levithan. Thanks to my sister, Erin, for her tireless work helping me keep all the facts straight; my brother, Ian, for just being you; my mom for always believing; and Matt for supporting me through all the ups and downs and keeping me sane when I start channeling Noelle or Ariana. Without you and our little ones, none of this would matter.

Finally, to all the YA librarians and independent bookstore owners who have worked so tirelessly to put good books in front of reluctant readers, my undying gratitude. Keep fighting the good fight, and I'll keep on writing!

*Cara agreed to help Zoe hide out—
no questions asked.
Isn't that what best friends are for?*

Elizabeth Woods's debut novel, *Choker*, will change
everything you thought you knew about friendship.
Learn more at **ElizabethWoodsBooks.com**.

EBOOK EDITION ALSO AVAILABLE

Seraphina's first love made her immortal . . .
Her second might get her killed.

THE
ALCHEMY
OF
FOREVER

BY

AVERY WILLIAMS

Find out more about Seraphina's forever life.
Visit TheAlchemyOfForever.com.